'**]**   a husky

Aching ...   blanking out
sensible thoughts. ...   Luke's kiss, and
her lips parted in breathless ...diness.

He drew her into his embrace and his lips
brushed her mouth in a tentative tease that sent
flames licking deep. And then Luke settled his
open mouth on hers and she sank helplessly
into him—into his warm, soft, slow kiss.

Five years. Five long years of separation and
loneliness. So long she'd waited. Too long.

'Erin,' he whispered again, making her name
sound beautiful, mysterious and special.

She lifted her hands to his shoulders and they
kissed deeply, tenderly, savouring each other,
letting layer upon layer of memory unfold, so
that this kiss felt like a part of every kiss they'd
ever shared. Sweet. Hungry. Poignant. Fierce.
Everything about Luke felt so right. She'd
known from the very first moment she'd seen
him that his arms were created to hold her. His
lips were designed for hers. How on earth had
she lost him?

Dear Reader

When I start to write a book I set out on a journey with my characters, never quite sure what lies around the corner or whether we'll safely reach our destination.

I begin each of these adventures with a bunch of 'what if?' questions, knowing that my desired destination is a happy ending for two people who are meant for each other.

But what if my characters have already tried marriage and failed? And what if there is a dearly loved, vulnerable child involved? And vast distances? What if this couple have very passionate natures that have caused them to make serious mistakes in the past? What if there has been a complete communication breakdown?

Many of my stories have ended with happy marriages in the Outback, but what if, this time, one of my characters simply cannot face the unrelenting isolation, the hardship and the danger of life in remote Australia?

These were the questions I began with when Erin Reilly and her son Joey met Luke Manning at Sydney airport.

Together with my characters, I took tentative steps into the mist, and over the weeks that followed this story emerged. I'm pleased to tell you that Erin and Luke proved to me once again that true love can find workable solutions to life's biggest hurdles. But the process is never easy. It takes courage and compassion—from all of us. I hope you enjoy their story.

Warmest wishes

Barbara Hannay

CLAIMING HIS FAMILY

BY
BARBARA HANNAY

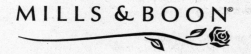

MILLS & BOON®

All the characters in this book have no existence outside the imagination of the author, and have no relation whatsoever to anyone bearing the same name or names. They are not even distantly inspired by any individual known or unknown to the author, and all the incidents are pure invention.

First published in Great Britain 2006
Harlequin Mills & Boon Limited,
Eton House, 18-24 Paradise Road, Richmond, Surrey TW9 1SR

© Barbara Hannay 2006

ISBN 0 263 84898 1

Set in Times Roman 13 on 14¾ pt.
02-0506-42896

Printed and bound in Spain
by Litografia Rosés, S.A., Barcelona

CHAPTER ONE

ERIN saw her ex-husband at the exact moment he saw her, at the very instant she emerged from Customs into the International Terminal at Sydney Airport. Their eyes met across the crowded sea of expectant faces, and she felt a jolt so savage she almost stumbled.

Luke Manning looked exactly as she remembered—a man who could never blend into a crowd. Wide-shouldered, long-legged and lean, with dark hair, prominent cheekbones and a mouth that could be brooding or good humoured by turns, Luke retained an air of inner confidence and calm that always set him apart.

But today there was something more. Despite the crowds that jostled him as they waved and called to loved ones, he gave an impression of remoteness, like the vast and lonely Australian Outback he loved.

Even at this distance his grey eyes could freeze her.

Erin drew a sharp breath. For a fleeting moment there had been a spark of excitement in Luke's eyes, but then, just as suddenly, the light vanished to be replaced with chilling blankness. In the past she'd never seen such coldness in his face, but its appearance now was hardly surprising. What else could she expect? Five years ago she'd walked away from their marriage. She hadn't seen him since.

Now she felt a flash of panic. Seeing Luke again was even harder than she'd feared.

She'd been schooling herself to feel nothing. Nothing. But all it had taken was that single icy glance from those too-familiar grey eyes and the wounds that were supposed to have healed were ripped open again.

Once again she felt the awful pain. This was what she'd dreaded, why she almost hadn't come.

A small, impatient hand tugged at hers. 'You said my dad would be here.' Joey sounded anxious. 'Can't you see him yet?'

'Yes, sweetheart, he's here.'

Erin gave Joey's hand a squeeze, more to reassure herself than her son. She tried to ignore the trembling in her stomach, the unwanted surge of anxiety shooting high, filling her throat.

Around them, the lines of fellow passengers were breaking up as weary travellers were enveloped by welcoming arms. Mere metres away, Luke Manning stood still, waiting.

Erin's heart thudded. She had to remember that this meeting was not about her. Or Luke. They weren't here to rake up the past. Neither of them wanted that. Their marriage was a closed book, finished for ever. They were meeting because of their son. This was for Joey, for his future.

She heard a sharp exclamation and felt Joey's hand slip from hers. He'd seen his father.

Even though Luke wasn't astride a stock horse or wearing an Akubra hat, he looked so like the photograph on Joey's nightstand that his son couldn't fail to recognise him.

'Hey, Dad!' Joey shrieked, and began to rush forward, but after three or four steps he stopped, overcome by shyness.

Erin, pushing the loaded luggage cart, tried
to catch up with the boy, but she too was
gripped by a vexing hesitation. It was like a bad
dream where she couldn't seem to move.
She'd come so far, all the way from Manhattan, but these last few steps seemed impossible.

Perhaps she should have accepted her
sister's offer to accompany Joey in her place.

How terrible this was. The three of them
were like a still-life tableau—Erin in her
trendy New-York black trouser suit, suitably
crease-resistant for travelling—Luke, an
Outback man in the city, in pale moleskin
trousers, a long-sleeved, blue cotton shirt
and carefully polished elastic-sided riding
boots—and little freckle-nosed, red-headed
Joey, staring up at his father as he clutched
his favourite possessions in a New York
Yankees backpack.

They stood there, stiffly silent and awkward
in the midst of the busy, bustling airport.

And then they seemed to come to life at
once. Luke's hands came out of his pockets
and his mouth quirked into a quarter-smile.
With his eyes fixed on Joey, he stepped
forward. Erin forced their luggage cart to

move once more. Joey hitched his backpack over one shoulder and grinned.

'Hi, Dad.' His face was glowing as he looked up at Luke.

'Hello, Joey.' Stooping low, Luke offered his right hand and Erin held her breath as she watched the man and the boy greet each other. She felt a leaping sensation in her chest as she saw the deep emotion in Luke's eyes, the shining pride in Joey's.

This was such a big moment for Joey—the culmination of months of longing and desperate impatience that had begun last autumn when he'd started school—when he'd suddenly become obsessed by a need to know everything about his father.

Now, as Erin watched, Luke's eyes seemed to devour the boy. What was he thinking? Was he remembering Joey's birth and how proud he'd been of his new baby son—how smitten they'd both been?

Was Luke looking for a physical resemblance to himself?

Superficially, Joey looked more like Erin's family, the Reillys. Both she and Joey had inherited dark red hair from her Irish father and their smallish noses were a Reilly feature too. But already it was clear that Joey was going to be tall like Luke and his high cheekbones were an unmistakable Manning legacy.

And the boy's eyes were smoky indigo, a true mixture of Erin's bright blue and Luke's deep grey.

She wondered if she should break the silence, but it was Joey who rescued the moment.

Shooting Luke a self-conscious grin, her son said, 'Good day, mate,' in his best attempt at an Australian accent.

Luke's face broke into a helpless crooked smile. 'G'day, little mate.' His voice sounded choked as his big brown hand ruffled Joey's buzz cut. Then he tapped the logo on Joey's backpack. 'How are the Yankees? Have they had a good season?'

Joey nodded shyly and then Luke looked in Erin's direction, his eyes bright yet wary.

Smile. She had to look cool and okay about this. Detached. *Smile, dammit.*

But her lips refused to curve and she was forced to tighten her cheek muscles until her mouth pulled outwards and upwards into a very mechanical grimacing smile.

Luke, on the other hand, didn't even bother to look pleased to see her. 'Hello, Erin.' His gaze was cold again and he spoke through tight lips.

'Hi, Luke.' She lifted her right hand, but then let it fall back onto the handle of the baggage cart. Best not to attempt to shake hands—it would be too embarrassing if Luke ignored her.

His jaw clenched, then relaxed. 'How was the flight?'

She shrugged. 'Very long.'

He nodded grimly.

Erin switched her attention to Joey, who was standing between them, and she stroked his cheek with her knuckles. 'This little tiger managed to sleep for eight hours, so he's ready and raring to go.'

'That's great.'

Joey's eyes shone as he stared up at Luke. 'Your cattle ranch is humungous, isn't it, Dad?'

'It's big.'

'As big as the whole of Texas?'

'Don't be silly, Joey.' Erin's voice sounded too tense but it couldn't be helped. 'You know it's not that big.'

'Well, it's bigger than Manhattan.' Joey giggled with the cheerful confidence of a kindergarten kid, not yet required to come to grips with geography.

'Quite a lot bigger than Manhattan,' Luke agreed. He turned to Erin. 'Let me push that cart for you.'

'It's okay. I'm managing.'

Overriding her foolishness, he stepped forward and his hand closed around her wrist. *Oh, help.* What was the matter with her? Did he notice how she almost jumped out of her skin?

For a breathless stretch of time he looked down at her small white hand, trapped by his, so large and brown. The contrast wasn't merely one of gender and size. The difference between Erin's sophisticated New York manicure and Luke's work-toughened, calloused palm signalled everything that had been wrong about their union.

'You've had a long flight and you're tired,' was all he said as he wrested the cart from her. 'Let's go. I'll take you to the hotel.'

Without another word, he turned abruptly and pushed the cart before him as he marched towards the escalators that led to the car park.

Joey hurried to keep up with Luke and after a small, somewhat weary sigh Erin followed.

'I wish we could go straight to your ranch, Dad,' Joey said as the escalator carried them to the floor below.

'You know that's not the plan.' Erin's tone held a tense warning. 'I told you Warrapinya is way up north near the top of Australia.' For Luke's benefit she added, 'I've explained to him that he'll be spending a day in Sydney first.'

She'd insisted on this. Heaven knew she wasn't looking forward to spending time with Luke, but she needed to discuss ground rules with him before he took off into the Outback. And she needed to observe how Luke interacted with Joey. No way was she going to hand her little boy over for two months in Luke Manning's care unless she was sure they would get along well.

'Can we fly all the way to your ranch?' Joey asked Luke.

'We certainly can.'

They reached the next floor and Luke hurried forward again. Joey was almost running to keep pace with his long stride.

'Do you really fly your own plane?' The boy's voice was squeaky with excitement.

'Sure do. I've just upgraded to a twin engine.'

'Oh, wow! That's so *neat*.' Joey's face was a picture of adoration.

Following behind them, Erin gnawed at her lip. It rankled that Luke had acquired a small plane and his pilot's licence after their marriage broke up. There'd been no planes available when she'd lived on Warrapinya and had desperately needed one.

But it was useless to dwell on what might have been. The marriage between the bride from Manhattan and the boss of Warrapinya had been doomed from the outset and it was only sensible to leave it where it lay. Discarded. Dead and buried.

As they headed out through automatic sliding glass doors and into the parking area Joey's piping voice and his endless questions added to her tension.

'Do you drive a pick-up, Dad?'

'They call pick-up trucks utes in Australia,' she snapped.

'Utes?' Joey pulled a face. 'That sounds weird.'

Luke grinned at him. 'We have lots of weird things down here.'

'Yeah.' Joey skipped excitedly. 'Do you have lots of weird animals on your ranch, Dad?'

'Plenty of roos. And crocs.'

'Crocs?' The boy came to an abrupt halt and his face paled visibly. 'Do you hunt crocodiles?'

Luke looked back over his shoulder and his grey eyes actually twinkled. 'Not before breakfast.'

'Joey's been watching that Australian television show about the crocodile hunter,' Erin explained.

She didn't add that he'd had several nightmares involving crocodiles and deadly snakes. Instead she slipped a comforting arm around her son. 'You're not too keen on crocodiles, are you, baby?'

Luke came to a stop and he frowned as he watched her fingers rubbing at Joey's shoulder. For some reason she felt suddenly self-conscious under his scrutiny and her hand grew still. Then she lifted it away and clenched it at her side.

'I hope you haven't made him into a sissy,' Luke said quietly.

'Of course I haven't.' Erin glared at him. 'That was uncalled for.'

Over Joey's head, their eyes fought a silent battle. And then there was a barely perceptible nod of Luke's head before he switched his attention back to the boy. 'Don't worry, mate. We'll keep well away from crocodiles while you're staying with me.'

They'd stopped near a long silver-grey sedan and, to Erin's surprise, Luke extracted a key from his pocket and pressed its central locking device.

She'd never seen Luke drive a city car before. Of course, he would have hired the car for the brief time he was in Sydney, but it was silly how little, unimportant things suddenly seemed to take on improbable significance. A sleek, sporty sedan didn't fit her image of Luke. Her memories of him involved uncomfortable, old and battered dust-covered utes, or sturdy four-wheel drives with clearance so high she'd almost needed a ladder to climb into them.

'Mom put stars and stripes stickers on our luggage so we could find it,' Joey commented proudly as Luke began to stow their suitcases into the car's trunk.

Luke straightened and let his gaze slide sideways to where Erin stood. 'That's a good idea,' he said, looking at her. 'Your mom's a very organised lady.'

Something bright—perhaps it was a trick of the light—seemed to flicker in his eyes and Erin felt a sudden need to plough nervous fingers through her hair.

Luke watched her action, his expression faintly worried. He was frowning as he closed the boot, and the frown held as he walked to open the front passenger door and motioned to Erin to take a seat.

Oh, help. The tension between them was suffocating, and it was only going to get worse if she had to sit there beside him.

'Can I sit in the front with you, Dad?'

For a beat or two Luke didn't seem to hear Joey, but then, with deliberate effort, he turned to the boy.

'Can I?' Joey persisted.

'You know children should always ride in the back,' Erin reminded him quickly.

'Your mother's right,' said Luke.

Joey pouted.

'I'll sit in the back with you, honey.' She didn't look at Luke so she missed his reaction to this. She took Joey's hand. She loved the touch of his still baby-soft skin and now she wanted to feel it again, to absorb the comfort of his small, warm hand clasping hers. Needing her.

More than ever she needed her son to need her now.

She and Joey had never been separated for more than a day or two, and that had only been when she'd been forced to take a short business trip. On those few occasions she'd left him with her mother, whose apartment was only two blocks away.

The thought of parting with her little boy for two long months was bad enough, but the reality of turning him over to the father he idolised was scary.

Going to Warrapinya would be a thrilling adventure for Joey. The Outback was astonishing, like nothing the boy had ever seen. Just the name Warrapinya stirred Erin, bringing a rush of memories of a unique and dramatic landscape—and good and bad reactions to match—at times a lift to her heart and at others a shudder down her spine.

She'd experienced the best and the worst of times there.

Joey, however, wouldn't see the problems. He'd love Luke's ranch. And he'd love Luke, who could be very charming and entertaining when he set his mind to it. She knew that only too well.

But…*what if*…what if Joey had such a great time with his dad that he didn't want to come back to her?

Oh, damn. She'd made a vow that she wouldn't give in to negative thoughts, and already she was letting her insecurities get the better of her. She had to stomp on them. Quickly.

Joey loved her. Erin knew that. She must never doubt it for a moment. They had a wonderful relationship full of love and easygoing warmth and companionship and fun.

Luke, she realised, was watching her again, but this time he'd schooled his features so there was no unsettling flicker and no chilling contempt. His gaze was devoid of emotion as he opened the car's back door for them.

'I've booked you into a hotel in Woolloomooloo, near the harbour,' he said as he closed the door, and then he slipped into the driver's seat and started the car.

It was late afternoon and the peak-hour rush had begun. Heavy, dull winter skies loomed. At home it was summer but down here in Sydney the people on the pavements were bundled inside coats and scarves and hurrying, as if eager to reach home and warmth. The threat of rain hovered, and in this dull light the city, famous for its bright and pretty harbour, looked unwelcoming.

But nothing could cloud Joey's happiness. From the back seat he leaned forward, straining against his seat belt so he could watch Luke.

Erin closed her eyes and let her head sink back against the luxuriously soft dove-grey leather upholstery. She felt exhausted, exhausted by the whole process of getting here, by the tension of it all, and the long flight followed by the tedious process of collecting their baggage, of making their way through Security, through Immigration and Customs.

Then the ordeal of seeing Luke again.

Oh, God. Without warning her mind flashed back to the last time she'd seen Luke, the day she'd left Warrapinya with Joey screaming in her arms.

It had been horrendous, the very worst thing she'd ever experienced. She'd relived it in her dreams a hundred times and each time she woke to find herself shaking and in tears. Even now she was falling apart just remembering.

She'd stood on the homestead veranda at the top of the front stairs, with her bags packed and tears streaming down her face, waiting for Nails, the Aboriginal odd-job man, who was going to drive her to the nearest airport at Cloncurry.

But, before Nails had arrived, Luke had appeared out of nowhere, charging up on a galloping horse and bearing an enormous bouquet of Outback flowers—golden wattle, red grevillea and purple wildflowers.

'What's going on?' he'd roared when he saw her suitcases.

Over Joey's cries she'd called back, 'I can't take any more of this place. I'm leaving you, Luke. Joey's sick and you've been gone for days and I've had enough.'

Luke had leapt from his horse. 'What's the matter with Joey?'

'I don't know. He just cries all the time and he won't feed.'

'I'll come with you. We'll take him to the doctor.'

'No, you don't understand. It's too late for you to try to help me now. It's over, Luke. I've had as much as I can take of this place. I'm going home and I'm taking Joey.'

At the time it hadn't felt like selfishness. She'd been on her own so much and she'd been so distraught about Joey. She'd been a nervous first-time mother and her baby had cried all the time, but the Flying Doctors hadn't considered her situation an emergency and her husband never seemed to be around. She'd felt she had no one to turn to.

Luke had been stunned. Unable to speak, he'd shoved the flowers at her. 'But I picked these for you.'

A tremendous heartbroken howl broke from her then as she swiped at his bouquet, making the colourful flowers spill from his hand and tumble down the steps. She'd been hysterical, she realised now, looking back.

'It's too late for flowers. There's no point.'

'But you can't leave.' The horror in Luke's

eyes had almost made her weaken. 'I don't understand.'

'Of course you don't understand. That's because you're never here. All I needed was a little support from you, Luke, but you just make a joke whenever I tell you how worried I am. And you've abandoned me here for weeks at a time. You're always off caring for your cattle. You've been gone all week, pulling cows out of bogs. Well, I'm bogged down here, but I'm getting myself out. I'm getting proper care for Joey and I'm not coming back.'

Nails drove up in the ute at that moment. Clutching Joey tightly, Erin fled down the steps and jumped into the front seat and locked the door.

There was been a terrible moment when Nails leaned out of the driver's window. 'You want to drive the missus into town, Boss?'

'No!' Erin cried. 'I don't want him, Nails. Come on, let's go.'

But Luke wasn't going to let her go without a fight. 'Hand over the keys, Nails. I'm taking my son to the doctor.'

Erin actually thought Luke might wrench the door open. 'You're too late!' she cried.

'Even if you follow me, you can't make me come back. I won't stay here.'

Luke glared at her, his eyes almost black with rage and despair. Jerking her head to the front, she stared ahead of her at the dusty track. 'Start the ute, Nails.'

And then Luke gave in suddenly. He threw her bags into the back of the vehicle and they landed with a heavy thump-thump. Completely bewildered, Nails shrugged, then depressed the accelerator and they left.

She would never forget the harrowing sound of Luke's angry voice shouting after them...

'Mommy, what's the matter?'

Joey was leaning forward, staring at her, and she realised that tears were streaming down her face. She forced a smile. 'It's nothing, Joey. I'm okay.'

'Don't you like Dad's car?'

'Yes, yes, it's fine. Your dad's a very good driver. I'm just a little tired.' She dug in her pocket for a tissue and wiped her eyes.

If only she could fast-forward the next twenty-four hours. She wanted to get this meeting and all that it involved behind her, and then she would be free to go off on her own holiday down under, and she would have nothing more to do with Luke Manning till August.

CHAPTER TWO

THE hotel Luke had booked for them was the height of luxury, much more upmarket than the hotels he'd been able to afford when he and Erin had been married. Overlooking one of the most scenic bays in Sydney Harbour, it was reminiscent of a grand nineteenth century home and furnished with beautiful antiques, oil paintings and fine tapestries.

Erin and Joey had a whole suite, with a sitting room, two separate bedrooms, glamorous bathrooms and French windows opening on to balconies with views across the water.

Joey was round-eyed with delight. 'Wow!' he shouted, running to the balcony to admire the busy spectacle of ships and ferries and sailing boats. 'This place is awesome, Dad.'

'Where are you staying?' Erin couldn't help asking Luke.

'Across the hall.'

There was a sharp edge to the way he said that and she wondered if his mind had followed the same direction as hers—recalling times in the past when they hadn't been able to keep their hands off each other, when they couldn't have borne to be separated by anything as vast as a hallway.

Don't be pathetic. Don't think about that.

'I'm sure you must be tired,' Luke added.

'Yes, I am a bit. A bath would be wonderful.'

'I'll leave you to settle in.' He glanced at his wristwatch. 'You won't want the ordeal of going to a restaurant this evening. I can organise room service if you like.' He spoke politely, but without warmth.

Erin found this emotionless, distanced Luke disturbing, almost formidable. She lifted her chin. 'Thank you, but you don't have to order for us. I'll take care of our meals.'

Luke frowned and his jaw clenched momentarily, but then he seemed to deliberately switch his attention to the open doorway of Joey's room. The little boy had suddenly run out of steam and he lay spread-eagled across the bed with his feet dangling over the edge, showing the soles of his trainers, criss-crossed with deep purple and black treads.

'Looks like Joey won't last much longer,' he said.

'He's fading fast. He's never flown before, so I'm not sure how he'll handle the jet lag.'

Without warning, Luke looked directly at her again, his grey eyes piercing cold. 'You said in your email that you had ground rules you wanted to discuss with me.'

'Oh…' To her annoyance she felt her cheeks grow hot. 'Yes, yes I do.'

'When would suit you?'

'I—er—I suppose it would be best to talk about them soon.'

'I could come back this evening per-haps—if Joey goes to sleep early?'

The thought of being alone with Luke, without Joey as a buffer, caused a hitch in her breathing, but it was best to get this over and done with. 'Okay. Give me an hour or so to get settled. Can you come around seven?'

'Right.'

As soon as Luke left Erin walked into Joey's room and he rolled on to his back and smiled up at her, his smoky blue eyes shining from beneath sleep-heavy lids. 'My dad's the best, isn't he, Mom?'

Was she strong enough to face Joey's rampant enthusiasm? 'Your dad thinks you're wonderful,' she said and she kissed him and sat very still on the edge of his bed, stroking his short, soft hair, aware as she'd been so many times before of the astonishing strength of her love for him.

Joey was the most important person, the most important *anything* in her life. Securing his happiness was her primary goal—for that she was risking this trip.

But letting him go was so scary. Once he got to know his father, he might never love her as completely or as perfectly as he did now. And she had no idea how Luke was going to react. Her one terror was that he might assume he had a right to reclaim his son.

But she couldn't allow herself to dwell on that or she would lose the plot completely. She had to take this one step at a time. Most importantly, she had to try to stay calm.

Forty-five minutes.

Erin had been back in Luke's life for less than an hour and he was a wreck.

In his hotel room he tossed his keys with such force they skimmed across the glassy surface of the bedside table and fell to the floor. He didn't bother to retrieve them.

He felt like hell.

His plan hadn't worked.

The plan had been to remain unmoved by the meeting with Erin and Joey. It should have been a cinch.

For the past five years he'd kept his feelings for his wife—his *ex*-wife—and her son safely locked away, buried deep, impenetrable, behind a walled fortress. He'd known there was no hope of saving his marriage, so he'd sentenced himself to five years' hard labour with no time off for good behaviour. He'd thrown himself into making Warrapinya the best cattle property in the north-west.

By the time Erin's letter had arrived, suggesting that he should meet his son, he had been sure he'd conquered his inner demons. He could handle a reunion without raising a sweat.

But at the airport just now, all it had taken was the first glimpse of Erin's bright autumn hair and her blue-as-heaven eyes and longing had ripped through him like a bullet.

Damn.

Luke marched to the window and stared grimly out without seeing the view. He had to get a grip. Surely he'd learned his lesson? How hard did a guy have to be slugged before he remembered that his marriage had been the biggest mistake of his life?

His shoulders rose and fell as he released a sigh of frustration. Okay, maybe he was never going to stop desiring Erin Reilly, but he was never going to do anything about it either. Erin was a no-go zone. No way was he going to make the same mistakes as last time.

As for the boy…

Luke was less certain about Joey. He had no idea what Erin had told their son about his father, about their marriage, but he'd been expecting the kid to see him as the bad guy. Joey's eagerness and excitement had knocked Luke for six. He didn't deserve his son's adoration, but it was there, shining in the boy's eyes.

Another very good reason to pull himself together.

Luke turned and caught his reflection in the mirror. He looked a shocker—face like dropped meat pie.

He forced a half-hearted smile. 'Cheer up, mate. Your ex might find you as appealing as a black snake in a sleeping bag, but your son thinks you're the duck's pyjamas.'

Erin should have been well prepared and calm when Luke strode back through her doorway an hour later, but she wasn't any kind of calm, and she had no one but herself to blame.

Too late, she'd realised that she'd spent far too long in the bath, and then she'd had to rush the business of blow-drying her hair and selecting something to wear.

When she heard Luke's knock, precisely on time, calmness wasn't even in the ballpark. Her short dark red hair was still damp and spiky and she'd had no time for make-up. Damn. She hadn't wanted to look dolled up, as if she was trying to impress the man, but she'd wanted, at the very least, to use some concealer to hide the traveller's puffy shadows under her eyes.

'Just a minute,' she called, angry with herself for not being ready and angry with Luke for being exactly on time. She snatched up her perfume. And then smacked it down again. It was Lost, the deeply sweet and

sensual scent she always wore. In the days
of their courtship and marriage Luke had
been crazy about it. Perhaps it wasn't wise
to wear it tonight.

There was another sharp tattoo on her
door. It sounded impatient. Bossy.

Annoyed, Erin grabbed the bottle again
and squirted the perfume at her neck, at her
wrists and into the V of her sweater. And
then, without bothering to hunt for her shoes,
she hurried to answer the door.

'I thought you must have fallen asleep,'
Luke said dryly.

'Is that why you were banging so loudly?'

'I wasn't banging.' A sudden flash of irri-
tation sparked in his cool eyes.

Oh, God. No doubt Luke was on edge too.
And they were fighting. Already.

Erin back-pedalled. 'I almost nodded off
in the bath, but I'd say I'm good for another
hour, tops.'

'I don't suppose our business will take
very long.'

'No, I guess not.' She waved a hand in the
direction of the armchairs arranged around
an elegant polished timber coffee table.
'Would you like coffee?'

'Not unless you'd like some.'

'I'm fine.'

They sat. Erin crossed her legs, but her bare feet and painted toenails seemed too—*naked*—and she wished she'd put shoes on. She uncrossed her legs again and tried, unsuccessfully, to tuck her feet out of sight. Luke settled comfortably with the ankle of one long leg balanced easily on the knee of the other.

It was daunting to be alone with him again after five long years. Everything about him was so familiar, and yet strange. There were changes too. He'd lost a little weight and gained a few lines. Resistance and stealthy watchfulness had replaced his easy good humour and ready smile.

His cool gaze slid over her, taking in her kitten-soft white cashmere sweater and sleek black Capri trousers—carelessly comfortable, elegant garments that she couldn't have afforded when they'd met seven years ago.

'No jewellery this evening,' he commented.

Surprised that he'd noticed, she lifted ringless hands to touch her bare throat and to finger her empty ear lobes. 'Too close to bedtime to bother.' *Besides, there's no one I need to impress.*

Watching her carefully, he hitched a casual arm over the back of his chair. 'So, how are things, Erin? How's your business?'

'Things are fine. My business is doing really well.'

'You're still in partnership with your sister?'

'Yes. And we've expanded. Angie and I still do all the designs, but we've taken on more staff to make most of our jewellery for us.'

It felt good to tell Luke that, to let him see that although she'd made a mess of her personal life, she was proud of her business success. 'Actually, we've just signed a contract with Candia Hart. Have you heard of her? She's one of the new big stars in Australian fashion design. She loves our stuff, and I'm meeting her here in Sydney to plan accessories for her show in New York next spring.'

Luke looked appropriately impressed. 'You'll be opening a shop on Fifth Avenue in no time.'

'You never know. We just might.'

'I had no idea there was such a high demand for coloured pencils threaded on string.'

Schmuck. Erin narrowed her eyes and waited for him to redeem himself with even the hint of a smile. In the past Luke's dry sense of humour had been one of his charms, but this evening there was no sign of it.

'We've expanded our repertoire,' she said tightly and then she lifted one hand in a sweeping flourish that took in the suite of rooms. 'Looks like your cattle business is doing well too. You're staying in five-star hotels these days, and buying twin-engine aeroplanes.'

He nodded, but offered no further comment. Instead he said, 'About these ground rules of yours.'

'Right.' Erin let out her breath with a nervous huff. 'I don't suppose they're rules exactly. Mostly, I wanted to fill you in a little. It's important we're both on the same page with the way we handle Joey.'

She paused then, hoping Luke might make a favourable comment about their son, about what a fine little guy he was, but he simply nodded grimly. His cool stare was a distinct challenge, but she was determined not to let him upset her.

'Fire away,' he said.

'Okay.' She pressed her lips together, and then released her breath again slowly. 'You'll get to know Joey better tomorrow, but I'm sure you've already noticed that he asks lots of questions.'

He nodded without smiling.

'You'll need to be prepared for that. Once you take him to Warrapinya he's bound to bombard you with questions—especially about—about us.'

'What about us?'

'About why we split up.' Lowering her gaze, she traced the pattern of tapestry leaves on the upholstered arm of her chair. 'I'm afraid he asks that question rather a lot—the same question over and over.'

'Why would he need to do that?' Luke asked sharply. 'Haven't you been able to give him a satisfactory answer?'

'I—I believe I have. I've certainly done my best.'

'But he keeps on asking—wanting to know why we spilt up?'

'Yes. He does it partly to learn, I guess, to

understand. But I think he's also checking that the answer stays the same.' She hurried on nervously. 'He can ask the most difficult questions at the most inconvenient moments. It always seems to happen to me when I'm standing in the supermarket line, or when I'm dropping him off at school.' And then, because Luke was looking at her with such clear dislike, she added, 'Or just as I'm about to go out and my date's standing on the doorstep.'

Luke's jaw stiffened and Erin felt a flicker of triumph, but then, as a dark stain tinged his neck, she almost wished she could take back that last cheap shot. She wanted her role in this meeting to be very mature, very civilised.

Shifting his weight slightly, Luke sat a little straighter and crossed his arms over his chest. 'Okay, so what is the answer, Erin?' He asked this very quietly, but the question seemed to reverberate around the room. 'What do you tell the boy about why we split up?'

An uncomfortable pulse beat at the base of her throat. 'I—I tell him the truth—that we weren't able to live together.'

'I see.' He stared at her. 'Is that all you've told him?'

'Pretty much. I've been careful never to criticise you, Luke.'

'Am I supposed to be grateful?'

Her teeth ground together and she took a deep breath, trying for an impossible calm. 'When Joey asks why we can't be a family, I remind him about what his teacher told the class—about all the different kinds of families there are.'

Luke frowned. 'For example?'

Was he being deliberately obtuse?

'Come on, Luke, you know as well as I do how many single and blended families there are these days. In America there are more children in those kinds of families than there are in families with both biological parents.'

'I'm sure that must be immensely reassuring for Joey.'

Sighing loudly, Erin thumped the arm of her chair. 'It's a fact of life.'

He sat very still, watching her.

'The important thing to remember is that Joey needs reassurance from both of us that we love him, that we're going to keep on

loving him even though we're separated—
even though—'

'Even though his parents don't love each
other,' Luke said, finishing the sentence in a
voice as dry as moon dust.

Erin felt as if she couldn't breathe. 'Yes,'
she managed at last.

There was another terrible silence while
they both stared at the floor.

'I suppose Joey must worry that you'll
leave him too.'

Her head shot up. 'No. He knows that's
impossible.'

'Does he?' Luke's glance was sharp and
hard. 'We were a family once. Joey's old
enough to realise that you must have loved
me once, but that didn't stop you from leaving.'

She leapt to her feet, needing to defend
herself, to swipe that stony accusation from
Luke's eyes. But she was trapped by his
ruthless gaze—like an escaping prisoner
caught in a searchlight's beam, her guilt
exposed. 'That's unfair and you know it.'

'It's plain logic, Erin. You said Joey's a
smart kid. Smart kids worry. I'm just trying
to see how the boy might view this.'

'Okay, I'll tell you how he views this. He loves me. I—I've been a good mom to him. I've been better than that. I've been great.'

'I don't think that's in question.'

'And he idolises you. I might be his mother, but you're his hero, Luke. He's got you on such a high pedestal you'll need a parachute to get down.'

Taken aback, Luke scratched the back of his neck. 'How did that happen?'

Erin shrugged. She was too tired and emotional to try to analyse the complexities of the absent father scenario now. 'Look,' she said. 'I've never said a word against you to Joey, and I need you to promise that you won't tell him things that will turn him against me.'

'Of course. I promise you have my word on that.'

She blinked hard as her eyes filled with sudden tears. 'Joey knows he'll be going back to New York with me at the end of this holiday.'

Luke made no comment.

'And—' She gulped; her throat had constricted over a knot of pain. 'I've made it very clear to him that there's no chance of us becoming a family again.'

'I see.' Luke stood abruptly and looked down at her from his too impressive height.

If only she'd put shoes on. Her bare feet were sinking into the deep pile of the carpet and, beside Luke, she felt too short. 'There's one last thing that's very important,' she said.

The line of his mouth tightened. 'What's that?'

'I want you to promise that you'll take really good care of Joey.'

Unexpected fury darkened his face. 'Of course I'll take bloody good care of him. How can you even ask that?'

'Who's going to look after Joey while you're off mending fences or shifting cattle?'

'I'll be with him all the time.'

'But—'

'My cousin is managing Warrapinya these days.'

'Really? I didn't even know you had a cousin.'

'Keith and his wife used to live on a station way out the back of Lake Nash, but these days Keith looks after the running of our place, so I'll be free to spend time with Joey.'

Erin stared at him, shocked. Luke's pro-longed ab- sences while he attended to the thousand and one jobs needed to run Warra-pinya had been a major cause of their break-up.

When she'd lived on Warrapinya it hadn't mattered how many employees Luke had—jackaroos, ringers or cooks—Luke had held himself responsible. He was the boss and the boss always went mustering, was always there for the tough work, the dirty work like fencing, dam building, branding, or breaking in horses. He'd maintained that he should take on the dangerous tasks rather than a worker.

If there was a wild scrub bull to be caught, it was the boss who led the way. Once a windmill's blades had gone berserk in a gale and the entire top threatened to tear off. Nails, the station handyman, had been going to climb up and disconnect the sails, but Luke had insisted on attending to it.

He'd claimed that running Warrapinya was more than a hands-on job. It was a hearts-on job.

Now it was beyond disconcerting to hear that in five short years Luke had delegated someone else to run Warrapinya for him. Joey would have his father's undivided attention. She should have been pleased, but instead she was fighting anger and hurt. 'I— I couldn't bear it if anything happened to Joey,' she said quickly.

'What's going to happen? What the hell are you talking about?'

'The Outback's so dangerous.'

With a groan, Luke flung back his head and stared at the ceiling. When he looked at her again, his eyes were blistering. 'You haven't filled Joey's head with that kind of bull, have you?'

'No.'

'I suppose you've told him that's why you left—because you were terrified of the Outback?'

'*No!*'

Jaw jutting belligerently, he stared at the toe of his riding boot and then flicked his gaze back to her. 'But that was it, wasn't it, Erin? It wasn't so much that we couldn't live together as that you couldn't live in the bush.'

There was no point in having this conversation. It was ancient history; their divorce was a *fait accompli*.

When Erin refused to answer, Luke took an intimidating step towards her.

With her shoulders braced, she said, 'You know it wasn't just that.'

'Okay…just to refresh my memory… what exactly was our problem?'

'For heaven's sake, it's not worth dragging that up now.'

'Come on, Erin, you can do better than that.'

'How can you ask now? It's too late.' Through clenched teeth, she added, 'It's *five* years too late.'

'I couldn't ask you five years ago. You ran away.'

'You didn't try to contact me after I left, Luke. You could have asked questions then.' Shaking with a deluge of anger and despair, she felt tears stand in her eyes. 'When I left Warrapinya, you yelled after me to go to hell. 'Good riddance', you yelled. And then, you never once tried to telephone me. There wasn't a word, Luke. You knew Joey was sick, but you never rang to find out how he was. Not once. You didn't want to know.'

Until she'd written to Luke to request a meeting with Joey he'd been silent. For five years he'd worn his stubborn pride like a badge of courage. The only contact had been via his lawyer and his accountant who supervised the regular deposits into her bank account for Joey's maintenance.

Now Luke stood facing her, his eyes bright with fury. A muscle clenched near his jaw line, but then he shook his head slowly. 'You're right,' he said. 'You're tired and jet lagged and this is the wrong time to try to discuss this.'

Without another word, he turned and strode quickly out of the room.

The door closed behind him and an angry sob rose in Erin's throat. She might have given way to tears, but there was a sound behind her and she turned to find Joey standing in the doorway of his bedroom, squinting into the light.

'Oh, sweetie,' she cried, arms outstretched as she hurried to him. 'Did we wake you?'

'You were shouting.'

'Shouting?'

'You and—and Dad.' He peered up at her and looked frightened. 'Are you crying, Mom?'

'No.' Hastily, she pulled Joey to her with

a one-armed hug while she sniffed and used her other hand to swipe at her eyes. She kissed the top of his head. 'Your dad and I were just talking. Sorry if we got a little loud.'

'You sounded mad.' Joey looked past her. 'Where's Dad now?'

'He's gone back to his room.'

'Why?'

'Because—because he needs to sleep. And so do I. So do you.'

'I'm not tired any more.'

Erin's heart sank to the floor. She was emotionally wrung out and dead on her feet. She couldn't bear it if Joey was wakeful now.

'I'll get room service to bring us some hot chocolate and something to eat,' she said. 'We'll have it together in my big bed and then you can snuggle up with me.'

The boy's bottom lip protruded as he thought about this. 'What can we have to eat?'

'What would you like?'

'Pancakes?'

'Pancakes at this hour?' Two seconds later, she shrugged. 'Why not? I'm sure the hotel can fix them for us. And then the sooner you get to sleep the sooner you'll see your dad in the morning.'

She was rewarded with a huge grin.

What exactly was our problem?

Why, Luke wondered, had he asked Erin that? After all, he'd had five years to come up with his own answers. He'd worked out exactly why their marriage had ended.

At the time, he hadn't seen it coming. There'd been no lead up. No storm warning.

It was only later that he'd understood that he should have taken Erin's concerns seriously. When she'd fretted about the baby he'd tried to jolly her out of it, had told her she worried too much.

When she'd got mad with him for spending too much time away working with cattle he hadn't tried to explain the pressures of running the property, he'd simply tried to shrug and crack a joke. Which had been pretty damn thoughtless. But he hated conflict.

If there had been a problem—a little bickering—he'd tended to say, 'Let's forget it and have a cuddle.' Erin, on the other hand, was a bit of a terrier. She was an up-front person. She wanted to push an issue through to the bitter end.

But tonight he'd been the terrier pushing her, goading her. Why the hell couldn't he stay calm and play this game her way? Their marriage was over.

Why was that so hard to remember?

What exactly was our problem?

Erin lay staring at the ceiling, desperate for sleep, while Luke's question echoed in her head.

How could Luke pretend not to know the answer? Their problem had been clear as day. Right from the start it had been there in letters ten feet high for everyone to see—everyone, that was, except the two of them, blinded by foolish, foolish passion.

Luke's parents and the Mannings' neighbours and the ranch hands—they had all known that Luke's Yankee bride was wrong for him. Her taste in clothes, her accent, her complexion, her attitude—everything was wrong.

The people at Warrapinya were friendly enough, but they had shown Erin, with varying degrees of subtlety, that she didn't fit in. Even the contract fencing team, who had spent a few weeks on the property repairing barbed wire fences, had looked at her with puzzled smiles and she knew they'd joked about her behind her back.

Even so, she felt so terribly, terribly guilty because the things that had ended their marriage were so small really. Luke hadn't gambled or drunk excessively or beaten her. But the little problems had snowballed till they loomed too large.

And that had been before Joey was born and her real problems started.

Everything had become completely clear once she had been safely back in New York. How could she ever have been so idiotic as to think she could live anywhere else?

CHAPTER THREE

THE scratch of a key turning in a lock woke Erin, but although she heard the sound quite distinctly she felt too drugged by sleep to respond.

She lay very still, drifting slowly up and up from the murky depths of deep slumber, aware of sounds…the rattle of the door opening and the thud of it closing. Then silence. Lovely. She could sink back into the mattress. She could…

Her eyes flashed open. Something was wrong. The silence was wrong. Was someone tiptoeing about in her room? An intruder?

Squinting through semi-darkness she saw unfamiliar furniture. The windows were covered by heavy curtains, but glimmers at either ends of the fabric indicated dazzling daylight outside.

Then she heard a loud whisper. 'Do you think she's awake yet?'

Joey.

Erin lurched upright, her heart racing as she remembered she was in a hotel in Sydney. How long had she slept? Oh, God, how long had Joey been awake? What had he been doing? Who was he talking to?

She flung the bedclothes aside just as two figures appeared at the door to her bedroom, one very tall, the other small.

'Mommy, you're awake!' A small, Joey-shaped torpedo launched across the carpet towards her. 'You've been asleep all day.'

'All day? I can't have.'

'Only half a day.' Luke's voice came from the doorway. 'It's just gone noon.'

Noon. Erin groaned. This day was the last time she had with Joey before he left for North Queensland. And she'd wasted half of it. Why hadn't she factored jet lag into her planning?

'We've already had breakfast *and* lunch,' Joey announced. ''Cause I was starving.' With a happy grin, he threw himself beside her on the bed. His cheeks glowed pink, as if he'd been running and playing outdoors. 'Guess what we had for lunch?'

Erin was super-aware of Luke watching from the doorway. Joey was sitting on top of the sheets so she couldn't use them to cover her bare legs. She tried to pull her yellow silk nightdress higher to cover the tops of her breasts. She hated to think how her hair must look. It would be a fright. She focused on Joey. 'I give up. What did you have for lunch?'

'Fish and chips,' he exclaimed excitedly. 'Dad and me had a picnic down near the water. We had these hot and crunchy pieces of fish with salty French fries and they were all wrapped up in paper.'

'Wow, that sounds…neat.'

'It was. It was excellent. And I fed some seagulls with little bits of my fish. And Dad and me had a soda too.'

With one hand holding her nightdress against her chest, Erin looked from her son to Luke. His eyes were bright and a smile lurked. She sensed a light-heartedness about him that she hadn't seen yesterday and she felt a perverse need to dampen it. 'You shouldn't have let me sleep in,' she accused.

'You were dead to the world.'

The happy light in his eyes flustered her

and she switched her attention back to Joey. 'So how did all this happen? When did you wake up?'

Joey shrugged. 'I heard Dad knocking on the door, so I opened it and let him in. And then Dad gave you a shake.'

'He what?'

Heat suffused her as she pictured what must have happened—Luke approaching her bed, leaning over her, touching her while she slept. Once more she flicked a hasty glance his way. He was still standing in the doorway, one shoulder resting casually against the frame, and she was annoyed to see a hint of amusement lurking in the depths of his smoky eyes.

Joey must have sensed her tension and he frowned. 'It was just a little shake, Mommy, but you didn't move. So Dad said we should leave you to sleep. He helped me to find some clothes and he wrote you a note and then we went out for breakfast.'

A note? It was then that Erin saw the page of hotel stationery on her nightstand and a message in Luke's sharp, spiky handwriting.

'So the two of you have spent the whole

morning together,' she said. 'I guess I should thank you, Luke.'

'Are you going to get up now?' prompted Joey. 'Dad said if you want, we can go to Taronga Park zoo.'

'Only if you're interested,' added Luke quickly.

Joey bounced excitedly, making the mattress rock beneath Erin. 'You want to go, don't you, Mommy? Dad said the zoo's on the other side of the harbour and we can get there on a ferry.'

Dad said, Dad said. Clearly Joey's adoration of Luke wasn't going to wane any time soon.

'You'll have to give me time to take a shower.'

'And you'll need coffee and something to eat,' added Luke, but his words were almost drowned out by Joey's cheers. 'Can I order something for you?'

Of course she said yes. She said yes to everything. There was no way she was going to let her dissent spoil this last afternoon with Joey. She even acquiesced when, as they left the hotel, Joey insisted on walking between them, holding her hand and Luke's as if the three of them were a regular family.

It was a beautiful day. As they boarded the bus bound for Circular Quay, Erin saw that yesterday's dull, threatening weather had cleared. The air was crisp and sparkling, the sky was a clean, bright blue and the sunshine had turned Sydney Harbour into a dazzling sea of sapphires. Although there was a nip in the air and they needed warm jackets, it was hard to remember that it was winter.

Joey found everything thrilling—even lining up to buy ferry tickets—and his happiness and excitement were catching. By the time the boat pulled away from the dock, Erin felt more at ease than she had in weeks. Perhaps, for one afternoon, she could keep her mind free from anxiety. She could aim to be as innocent and carefree as Joey.

Luke was in a better mood too, so perhaps they could all relax. She decided to try very hard. She would live in the moment and immerse herself in the simple enjoyment of the sunshine, the sparkling harbour and the freshness of the salty breeze skimming across the water.

For just one afternoon, they could all pretend that everything was okay.

It was a nice theory.

It couldn't work, of course.

The happy-family charade was too fragile to withstand the test of an entire afternoon. Minute by minute—while Erin and Luke laughed at the antics of the monkeys, while they waved to Joey as he rode an elephant on a merry-go-round, while they shared his admiration of the lions and tigers and his amusement over the cute little meerkats— the tension between them mounted.

Whenever Joey let go of their hands and danced ahead of them, Erin walked carefully apart from Luke, taking excessive pains not to touch him or bump him. And they were both excruciatingly careful to pay attention to Joey and to show an intense fascination with the animals on display. They took the same care to pay little or no attention to each other.

And gradually the light-hearted glimmer in Luke's eyes dimmed and Erin's smile became more strained.

If Joey noticed their apprehension he didn't let on. This afternoon was too important to him. For the first time he could remember he had both his parents together. He was living his dream and it was almost as if he were willing Erin and Luke to be on their best behaviour so they couldn't spoil his happiness.

And Erin and Luke were managing tolerably well. On the surface. Things deteriorated when they reached the kangaroos.

Kangaroos were so bizarre, Erin thought, with their soft, pretty faces, their tiny front paws and then their absurdly long back legs. Bizarre, but very cute. She pointed out a sweet little baby in its mother's pouch.

Joey was entranced. He clung to the wire with his face pressed against it as he watched the baby kangaroo's little black eyes, pointed nose and ears peeping out from a furry pocket on its mother's abdomen.

'Did you know that baby kangaroos are called joeys?' Luke asked him.

Joey pulled back from the wire to stare up at them with excited delight. 'Is that why you guys called me Joey, 'cause I'm *your* baby?'

'Well…not exactly,' Erin began and then she winced. Why had she chosen this moment to become pedantic?

Joey waited expectantly for further explanation.

'Your name's short for Joseph,' she said. 'You were named after your grandfather.'

'After Grandpa Reilly?'

'No, your other grandfather.' Erin glanced towards Luke and a nervous tremble rippled through her as she watched a muscle twitch near his jaw. 'His name was Joseph too,' she said. 'He was Joseph Manning—just like you.'

'The first Joseph Manning was my dad,' Luke explained. 'We called you Joseph Peter. Joseph after my father and Peter after Peter Reilly, your mother's father.'

Luke's words were addressed to Joey, but he fixed his eyes directly on Erin and she felt heat spread like a sunrise up her neck and into her face. She knew Luke was remembering that day when they'd chosen Joey's names—when they'd been so overjoyed, so proud and grateful, so pleased with themselves. They'd been overflowing with love— for each other, for their son, for their parents, for the whole world.

'Wow!' Joey was saying now. 'So you and Mommy both gave me a name each.' He seemed exceptionally pleased with this news.

Luke cleared his throat and looked away.

'What would you like to see next?' Erin was eager to change the subject.

But Joey was not to be deterred. Reaching for Luke's hand, he gave it a little tug. 'Were you there, Dad, when I was born?'

Again, another visible clenching of the muscle in Luke's jaw. 'Yes...yes I was there.'

'In the hospital?'

'Yes.' Luke looked down at Joey and his face twisted suddenly.

Erin couldn't bear to see his sad, lost expression. The sight made her panic. But then Luke's mouth broke into a rueful grin and he gave Joey's crew cut a playful scuff. Holding his hands apart in front of him, he said, 'You were only this big, but you made so much noise I needed ear plugs.'

Joey laughed and wrapped his arms around Luke's legs, hugging him hard. 'Did I hurt your ears?'

'Sure. You were like a little frog, with arms and legs waving madly, and then you went red in the face and bellowed your lungs out.'

'Then what happened?'

Luke hesitated and he sent Erin a quick searching glance. Oh, God. His eyes were so full of pain. Her knees threatened to cave in as she remembered how Luke had been on that night when Joey was born—the raw emotion, the sheer elation.

'What happened?' Joey asked again and she wondered if he was aware of their tension. Was the boy manipulating them?

'Your mum was tired,' Luke said. 'So the doctor handed you to me and I was worried because you were so tiny and squirmy and I thought I was going to drop you.'

Joey giggled. 'Did you drop me?'

'Course not.'

'And then what happened?'

Luke smiled so unhappily Erin thought her heart might break.

'After that,' Luke said with his gaze fixed on Erin, 'your mother looked up at me and she was so happy her eyes were as bright as stars. She thought you were the most beautiful baby ever born.'

Over Joey's head Luke watched Erin. His eyes were brimming with a powerful emotion she couldn't identify. Was it anger, regret…or something else entirely?

A happy little huffing sigh broke softly from Joey's lips. He took Luke's hand and reached for Erin's.

No one in the trio spoke as they began to walk forward again. Each seemed to be locked in private thoughts.

Erin was horrified by hers.

The trip back to the hotel by ferry and bus was an ordeal. Joey was beginning to droop, and Erin was withdrawn. Conversation was limited to essentials.

Luke sat stiffly apart from them, wrestling with doubts.

Nothing was working out the way he'd expected. He'd been steeling himself for a battle with Erin. He'd expected Joey to be wary and that he'd have to win him over. Instead Erin was timid and jumpy around him and Joey thought he was Superdad. In the boy's eyes he couldn't put a foot wrong.

And looking at Erin was driving him crazy. He just wanted to stare into her eyes all the time. He'd swear they were still the bluest eyes he'd ever seen. But it wasn't only her eyes, of course. Her hips and her legs were worthy of close observation too. And he loved the way her hair was cut so it lay in feathery wisps against the back of her neck.

And he kept remembering the rest of her...

There was no mention of the three of them having dinner together, and once they reached the hotel Erin became very business-like.

'So you'll want to get away early in the morning?' she asked Luke.

'Yes. I've booked us on a flight to Brisbane and then we'll take my plane from there.'

'How early do you want to leave? Six?'

'Seven will be fine.'

'Okay, Joey will be ready at seven. I'll organise a wake-up call and an early break-fast. I'll repack his bag tonight. There'll be some clothes that will need washing. I'll keep them separate in a zip-lock bag.'

She drew a deep breath and looked down at her hands, nervously twisting a set of three hand-engraved silver and turquoise rings back and forth on her finger. 'Joey's had a lovely day today.' She lifted her gaze. 'He's really going to enjoy his time with you.'

Luke's eyes shimmered. 'I'll take good care of him, Erin.'

'Yes.' She blinked. Twice. 'Yes, I know you will.'

When he left, she closed the door to their suite quickly and became very brisk, bustling Joey into the bath, ordering a simple meal from room service and sorting Joey's clothes. She was terrified that she would start to cry, but she couldn't, she mustn't.

Joey mustn't guess how she was feeling. Damn it, she was so mixed up she didn't really know how she was feeling.

At bedtime Joey said, 'I wish you could come to Warrapinya, Mommy.'

'You don't need me there,' she said quickly. 'You're going to have a great time with your dad.'

'But why can't you come too? Dad would let you come, wouldn't he?'

'That's not what we've arranged, Joey. And I have business here in Sydney that will keep me busy.'

Joey pouted and punched his pillow. 'I don't get it.'

'What don't you get?'

'Why you don't like Dad.' He looked up

at her with pleading eyes. 'He's the greatest. Why can't you like him, Mommy?'

'It's—it's complicated.' Erin bit her lip. 'Luke's a good man, Joey. A—a very nice man.'

The boy waited and his dubious scowl told her she was doing a lousy job of explaining. But how could she destroy his innocence by telling him that love wasn't always enough? She tried again. 'When a mommy and a daddy decide they don't want to be married any more, it means they—they don't want to spend too much time together.'

'But why? Don't you like that mushy stuff—like kissing and going to bed together?'

'Joey!' Erin couldn't hide her shock. 'Where did you hear that kind of talk?'

The boy shrugged. 'Kids talk about married stuff sometimes.' Then he looked at her eagerly. 'If you don't want Dad to kiss you, maybe you could just tell him and then he'd say that's okay, and you could come with us anyhow.'

Thrilled with his brilliant idea, Joey launched out of bed. 'Why don't we go and tell him?'

'No!' Erin shrieked.

'Well, I can tell him for you.'

'No.' Grabbing his arm, she shepherded him back beneath the bedclothes. 'Sweetheart, you don't understand. Your dad wouldn't enjoy having me back at Warrapinya.'

'Bet he would. Have you asked him?'

'I'm not going to, Joey. Don't keep on about it. It's just not going to happen.' With her fingertips, she stroked the pink curve of his ear. 'This is a "boys only" adventure, just for you and your dad,' she said.

In the morning Joey was so excited he leapt out of bed the minute the wake-up call rang through, and while Erin was still fumbling sleepily with the coffee-maker, he dressed, without help, in record time.

Everything happened in a flash—the business of breakfast, of cleaning teeth and checking for stray socks and Joey's Game Boy under his bed, of zipping his suitcase and setting it near the door.

In no time Joey was ready and Erin was opening the door to Luke.

Her heart did a kind of somersault when

she saw him, and she wished that it wouldn't. She didn't want to feel anything for Luke. It would spoil everything if she got silly.

'There's no point in my coming to the airport,' she said, keeping her gaze no higher than his broad shoulder. 'I'll say goodbye here.'

She knelt beside Joey and gave him a hug and a kiss and then another hug. Joey clung to her and she could feel his little body trembling with excitement and just a little fear. 'Daddy's going to take good care of you,' she whispered. Then she said more brightly, 'You can call me when you get to Warrapinya. I'll expect to hear all about your adventures.'

The boy nodded against her shoulder and she gave him one more kiss, a final hug.

'I love you,' she whispered and then she stood. Her eyes met Luke's and she felt another flash, another unwanted leap of excitement. She forced a smile. 'I packed a photo album in with Joey's things. It's for you. I had copies made of all the best ones. Of Joey. You know. All the milestones.'

'Thanks.' His voice sounded rough around the edges.

'You'd better get going,' she said, keeping her chin bravely high.

'Indeed.' With two fingers he snagged Joey's suitcase.

Erin opened the door. 'Have a great trip now.'

The man and the boy passed through the doorway.

'Bye, Mom.'

'Bye, Joey-boy.' Erin swallowed to push away the sharp lump in her throat.

Luke was watching her closely and she realised with a pang that no matter how hard she tried to deny it she was going to miss him, too. The little light inside her would go out when he left.

And then he set down the suitcase. 'I'd better say goodbye, too.'

Before she had time to understand what was happening, his hands were at her waist and he was kissing her.

Within seconds she was trembling beneath the unexpected warmth of his lips.

Over the past five years she had tried so hard to forget what Luke's kiss was like, had tried to block from her mind the physical desire she'd always felt for him. But she'd been fooling herself. One touch of Luke's lips on her and her skin was aflame. Longing burst inside her like a flower coming into bloom.

'No!' Joey's voice shouted beside them. 'No, Dad, stop it. Mommy doesn't want you to kiss her. She told me.'

With a sharp groan, Luke lifted his head. His arms released her as quickly as he'd embraced her and he stepped away.

Stunned, flushed and breathless, Erin sagged against the door frame.

'Are you all right, Mommy?' Joey looked worried and he touched her hand.

She took a quick breath and nodded, then squeezed his fingers to reassure him. 'Yes, sweetheart, of course I'm okay. I'm fine.'

Her eyes sought Luke's, but he was already bending to retrieve the suitcase. When he straightened, she saw that his face was flushed and his eyes were burning beneath stern brows. He stood very stiffly and gave her a curt nod, and then turned to the boy. 'Are you ready, Joey?'

'Yeah, sure. I've been ready for ages.'

'Then we'd better be on our way.'

Now they were heading down the hall and

Joey flashed Erin one last searching glance over his shoulder.

She waved and smiled fiercely to show him she was fine.

'I don't know why Mom doesn't want you to kiss her, do you, Dad?' she heard Joey ask, and she knew that Luke said something in reply but she couldn't hear his answer.

It must have been flippant because, as she watched, Joey laughed and then he gave a little skip and he took his father's hand and then they turned the corner and disappeared.

CHAPTER FOUR

LUKE stared out through the passenger jet's porthole and sighed. Beside him Joey was absorbed in a colouring book, but Luke couldn't stop thinking about Erin. And that kiss.

Why the blue blazes had he kissed her?

Oh, come on, man. As if you don't know.

He might as well admit the truth. He'd been fantasising about kissing her ever since he'd seen her asleep yesterday. Maybe he'd been thinking about it since he'd seen her at Sydney Airport, but yesterday in bed she'd looked so lovely and soft and warm, and the thin silk strap of her yellow nightie had slipped off her shoulder, and he'd burned with the need to touch her.

How could he help it? His head was

stuffed to overflowing with memories of her. In bed. In bed with him.

But what was truly blowing his mind now was the knowledge that Erin had wanted the kiss as much as he had. From the instant he'd taken her into his arms he'd sensed it. And then he'd felt the warm eagerness of her lips opening beneath his, her willingness as she'd looped her arms around his neck and as she'd melted into him. Oh, man, she'd felt good.

But then Joey had started yelling that Erin didn't want to be kissed. The boy was wrong.

He hadn't a clue.

Even so, Luke regretted the kiss. In his head, he regretted it. His heart was another matter, but that didn't count.

What counted was the unpalatable truth. The kiss had been another mistake. He and Erin were no longer husband and wife and nothing was going to change, so there was no point in even thinking about it.

It was a good thing, a very good thing, that he and Erin were going to be separated by hundreds of kilometres for almost two months.

* * *

As soon as Luke left with Joey an awful feeling of emptiness invaded Erin. An aching loneliness. She turned back into her hotel room feeling lost and abandoned, as if she'd been set aside, discarded.

How could she bear it? Letting Joey go had broken her heart. He'd looked so tiny and vulnerable as he'd disappeared down the corridor, hand in hand with Luke.

And Luke. What on earth was she to make of him? Why had he kissed her?

If he'd wanted to remind her of the passion that had once been front, back and centre of their lives, he'd been successful. But why? He'd looked so upset afterwards, as if he'd known he'd made an impulsive mistake. Again.

She was sick with confusion.

Opening the French doors that led to the balcony, she stepped into sunshine and drew a deep breath of fresh air, and then another. The sky was a beautiful clean blue, as if it had been thoroughly washed, rinsed with fabric softener and hung out to dry—a gorgeous day for flying.

Oh, help. She felt a swift clutch of panic at the thought of Joey in that tiny plane with

Luke, flying all the way north across Queensland. It was such a long journey for a small plane.

Be safe, little man. She would never forgive Luke if he let anything—

No, it was silly to even think of it.

She needed to shut off thoughts of Joey and Luke. They would be gone for almost two months and she would drive herself crazy if she worried the whole time. She had to make an effort now to put them out of her mind.

This was going to be *her* time—time for her business, for networking, for revitalising her creativity by indulging in sightseeing trips, visits to art galleries and fashion houses. Down-under designers had a unique view of the world and she wanted to broaden her own perspective.

And then, after she'd spent some time in Sydney and Melbourne, she was going to rent a little cottage at the seaside. Over the Internet she'd found just the thing at Byron Bay and it was going to be her special treat to herself. She was planning to relax completely and to dabble in whatever creative whim took her fancy—jewellery design, a little landscape painting perhaps and maybe some collage using objects she found beach-combing.

With her hands resting on the sun-warmed balustrade she let her head fall back. Morning sunlight streamed over her face. She steadied her breathing and fixed her mind on the pleasing image of a smooth white beach and a gentle sun, a shimmering sea, cheerful little waves lapping and a solitary cloud floating...floating...

In the bedroom behind her, her cellphone rang.

She jumped. And her first thought was of Joey. Was there a problem? Was he missing her already? Perhaps the call was from Luke. Joey was in tears and Luke didn't think he could cope.

Oh, how silly she was. As she dashed back into the bedroom she scolded herself. *Snap out of it. Joey's safe with his father. Get used to it.*

But her hand was trembling as she snatched her cellphone from the nightstand. Primed to hear Luke's voice, she asked nervously, 'Hello?'

'Hey, sis.'

'Angie? Is that you?'

'You got another sister you never told me about?'

Erin was almost smiling as she sank on to the edge of the bed. 'Oh, Angie, it's so good to hear your voice. But what time is it there? Shouldn't you be asleep?'

'Ed was called out to a fire and I couldn't get back to sleep, so I thought I'd call you. Are you okay? You sound upset.'

'I am a bit. But it's only because Joey's just left for the airport. He went off with Luke five minutes ago.' She pressed a hand to her mouth.

'You're missing him already.'

'Yes.'

'Oh, Erin, I wish I could hug you.'

The sisterly concern in Angie's voice was almost the undoing of Erin. It took every ounce of her will-power not to burst into tears.

'Does Luke understand how hard this vacation is going to be for you?' Angie asked. 'Did you tell him you've never been separated from Joey?'

'Luke's been separated from Joey for five years, so I couldn't exactly make a fuss.'

'Well, yeah. I guess there's that.'

'And I don't want Luke to think I'm turning Joey into a momma's boy. He's already alluded to that.'

'*Ouch.* Not fair.' Angie let out a noisy, sympathetic sigh. 'So how *is* the cowboy?'

'He's—he's well.'

'Erin, you know I wasn't enquiring about his health. How's his attitude?'

'He's—' Erin hesitated. What could she say about Luke? 'He's very good with Joey. And Joey is wrapped up in him, of course.'

'That's a relief. How has he treated you, Erin? Has he been civil? He hasn't given you a hard time, has he?'

'No, he's been—fine.'

'Fine? What's that supposed to mean? Give me details, woman.'

'He's—he's been reasonable and cooperative and he's agreed to my terms. I suppose you could say he hasn't put a foot wrong.' The placement of Luke's lips was another matter, but no way was she going to tell Angie about that kiss. 'How's Ed?'

'Ed's just dandy. Now, back to Luke. Is he still a hunk?'

'Oh, Angie, why ask?'

'I'm curious.'

'He—he looks much the same.'

Angie didn't respond immediately and in the uncomfortable silence Erin silently cursed her sister's uncanny ability to tune in to her secret thoughts—because right at this moment Erin's thoughts couldn't let go of how *hunky,* how exactly right Luke looked.

She couldn't help it. There was a part of her that would always be in love with the way Luke Manning looked. In many perplexing ways she still felt so essentially connected to the man that the five years of separation made no difference.

Seeing Luke again had awoken all the feelings she'd desperately tried to bury. Just being in his company had almost blinded her to their problems. In the past twenty-four hours there'd been dangerous moments when she'd wondered, she'd almost wished...

No.

No, no, no. She was simply feeling vulnerable today after saying goodbye to Joey. 'The weather here's just gorgeous,' she said.

'Erin, it's your sister you're talking to. When you start delivering weather reports on an international call I know you're stalling. Come on, what was it like to see Luke again after all this time? I bet there's still a spark.'

'There were no sparks,' Erin snapped.

'Okay, okay. No need to bite my head off. But don't be surprised if romance is in the air. You have Venus in your sign this month.'

'Oh, Angie, give up.'

Another silence. 'So what's the problem, honey?'

'I told you, I'm missing Joey. But don't worry, I'll get over that in a day or two.' Erin wiped her eyes with the back of her hand. 'I'm moving into another hotel that's even closer to everything I want to see and I've planned a bunch of interesting things to do here in Sydney.'

'Sounds good,' Angie said gently. 'Just promise me one thing.'

'What's that?'

'Don't fall in love with another Australian.'

A startled, hiccuping laugh burst from Erin. 'I promise, I swear. There's no chance of making that mistake again.'

'Yeah, there's only one Aussie for you.'

'*Angelina!* That's a totally pathetic thing to say.'

'Sorry. I won't utter another word on the subject. I guess I'd better end this call anyhow.'

'Okay. Thanks for calling. Give my love to Mamma and to Ed.'

'Sure. Ciao, Erin.'

'Ciao.'

Erin hung up, thinking of home. She thought about her mother, Lucia Lancantore Reilly, a silver-haired dark-eyed woman who was still so beautiful at sixty that men of all ages turned in the street to take a second look. But, as far as Erin knew, her mother had never let another man into her life, after her husband.

Did Mamma ever miss their charming, handsome, raconteur father? Fifteen years ago Peter Reilly had returned to Ireland when his brother had died. He'd stayed on to help run the family farm for a bit, but he'd loved it so much he'd wanted to stay, and although he'd begged Lucia to join him she'd stubbornly refused to leave Manhattan.

But if her mother had regrets she'd never shared them. Lucia had always shrugged

Erin's questions aside as silly or annoying, claiming that the answers were nobody's business but hers.

Lucia claimed she was perfectly happy with her job as a doctor's receptionist, her church around the corner and her bridge club friends with whom she went to the movies on Saturdays and walked in Central Park between six and seven each weekday morning.

But are you really happy, Mamma?

'I knew you wouldn't last in Australia,' her mother had said when Erin had returned from her marriage, broken-hearted. 'You're too much like me. You can't change.'

Why hadn't Erin seen that for herself?

The answer, of course, was Luke Manning. On a fine summer's day in New York she'd taken one look at him and she'd discovered the astonishing, illogical, life-changing power of love. Not mushy love, but the real thing. Knowledge too deep for words. An overwhelming force that defied logic.

She could remember every detail of the fateful day she met Luke. Thinking about it now, she could see it all.

She'd been in Times Square on a bright summer's day, mid-morning, on her way to a meeting with Angie and an important new client. As she'd crossed Seventh Avenue she'd been annoyed to find the pavement completely blocked by a crowd gathered around some guy wearing little more than a cowboy hat and strumming a guitar.

Erin had needed to press on and she'd taken a quick step backwards to bypass a cluster of grinning tourists. And she'd bumped into someone close behind her—someone hard and muscly.

'Oh, excuse me.' Turning briefly, she flipped a businesslike smile over her shoulder.

And that was when it happened.

The sultry summer morning, the almost-naked strumming cowboy, the honking traffic, the crowd and Erin's pressing appointment ceased to exist.

She was looking into a man's face and was compelled to stand stock-still.

And stare.

He wasn't drop-dead handsome exactly. But everything about him—*everything*—spoke to her. The clean-cut manliness of his face, the smiling warmth in his eyes, the healthy sheen on his short brown hair, his hard-packed leanness, his height—

Right then, in a New York split-second, Erin knew that her life had entered a new dimension of fabulousness.

A voice deep inside her whispered that this man was *it*—the answer to a secret question she'd been asking since she was eleven years old, when she and Angie had knelt at their bedroom window and looked out across the crowded Manhattan skyline to send girlish wishes into the night.

This man was the one.

He was meant for her.

Even his clothes—simple blue jeans and a white cotton shirt with the sleeves rolled back over his forearms—were perfect.

Erin couldn't move.

And it looked as if he couldn't either. He was staring at her so intently that he seemed as stunned as she was. He opened his mouth to speak but nothing came out and then he shook his head and he offered her a shaky grin.

And finally, when he did speak, it was little more than a whisper. 'Are you real?'

Erin gulped. 'I beg your pardon?'

'I'm sorry, it's just that I've never seen anyone with such amazing blue eyes. Your eyes are so beautiful. Are they real?'

It was either the corniest come-on line in the history of guys meeting gals, or it was a wonderfully genuine compliment.

As a New Yorker, Erin was too streetwise and sophisticated to let some strange man sweep her off her feet, so she played it safe. She treated his remark as a kind of joke. 'What do you take me for? Of course my eyes aren't real.'

'I thought they were too blue to be true. So what's the trick? You're wearing tinted lenses?'

It was only then that Erin recognised his Australian accent. Alarm bells rang.

Darn. He wasn't a New Yorker—not even an American. Her vibes had been way off the mark. This man couldn't possibly be meant for her after all.

She loved her home town and she couldn't imagine living anywhere else. She had no intention of falling for a tourist. She didn't plan on getting interested in any man who lived as far away as Mississippi, let alone Australia.

Disappointment sluiced through her. But how crazy was that? What was the matter with her? How could she get so instantly worked up about a stranger—in Times Square, for heaven's sake? She was normally quite level-headed, about guys. Too level-headed, Angie always claimed.

She offered the handsome Australian a parting shrugging smile and turned, about to head off down West 47th Street. But, with a neat side-step, he quickly blocked her.

'Just a minute—*please.*'

If any other guy had blocked her way she would have told him to step aside unless he wanted to find himself down on the pavement. She'd learned some sharp moves in self-defence classes. But somehow even this guy's intrusion into her personal space charmed her.

'Excuse me,' she said meekly, taking another step. 'I have to get going.'

He didn't hesitate to block her way again. 'You can't rush off.'

'I can too. I have a meeting.'

'Are you sure about that?'

Huh? 'Well, yes, of course I'm sure.' She gave an impatient roll of her eyes.

His gaze held hers.

Oh, God. There was something so wonderfully *right* about him—a kind of ruggedness that was manly without being rough, a toughness that would never be mean. And there was intelligence and a spark of humour in his eyes, and then there was his sexy smile. His smile sent shivers dancing through her.

'I don't think you should go,' he said.

'But I have to.'

With an outstretched arm he made a sweeping gesture that took in the crowds on Seventh Avenue and the towering buildings all around them. 'Think how many hundreds of meetings are taking place right now, all over New York City. Surely it won't matter if one person misses just one of them.'

It wasn't a logical argument and she wanted to protest. She *should* have protested. She tried, but the words died on her lips.

'There's something more important that you've got to do,' he said.

'W-what's that?'

'Have coffee with me.'

She felt her jaw drop. 'Are you serious?'

'Absolutely.'

Of course she was surprised. And pleased. But she ignored the little voice inside her shouting, *yes, yes, yes!* 'How can coffee with you be more important than a business appointment?'

For long seconds he didn't answer and she almost wished she hadn't asked, because there was only one correct and sensible answer and it wasn't what she actually wanted to hear. But then his sexy mouth curved into another brain-melting smile.

'We should have coffee now because this city is so huge and frantic that if I let you go I might never see you again. This could be the one and only chance we'll ever have to get to know each other.'

Oh, help.

'And I think we really should get to know each other.'

Oh…help! Deep in her bones she was sure that he was right.

He managed to frown and smile at the same time and Erin couldn't help smiling back. Next minute they were swapping proper introductions and then they were heading down the pavement to the nearest diner and Erin was calling Angie on her cellphone to tell her she couldn't make it to their meeting.

'Something's come up,' she said.

'What kind of something?'

'Something urgent.'

She heard her sister's suspicious groan. 'I've just spent nearly an hour on the bus and the subway to get here.' Angie had moved to Queens when she married her fireman husband, Ed.

'You can show our designs to Mario. You don't need me, Ange.'

'This had better be a matter of life and death.'

'It is.' Erin knew she didn't sound at all convincing.

There was an eloquent pause from Angie and then... 'Oh, my gosh, it's a guy.'

Erin winced, but didn't reply.

'I'm right, Erin. I can tell. It is a guy, isn't it?'

'I'll call you soon, Angie.'

'Is he with you now? Is he gorgeous? He must be divine. I know you, sis. You wouldn't cancel unless he was a *god*.'

'I'll call you.' Erin snapped her cellphone shut, cutting Angie off mid-scream. Then she noticed that her companion was also making a call on his phone.

'Yeah, mate, I'm really sorry,' he was saying. 'I'll get back to you.' As he finished and slipped the cellphone into the back pocket of his jeans he caught the curiosity in Erin's eyes and he shot her a cute guilty smile.

She shook her head at him. 'Don't tell me you had to cancel a meeting too?'

'Just a writer bloke who knows an agent. I'll catch up with him another time.'

'You're a writer?' *How interesting.*

He shrugged. 'Not really. Nothing serious.'

'So, what do you do?'

Luke told her.

Oh, my gosh.

Oh... my... God. Erin couldn't hold back a gasp of dismay. 'A cowboy?' How on earth could she be even remotely interested in a cowboy?

Luke shot her a wary sideways glance. 'They don't call us cowboys in Australia.'

'But you ride horses and you wear a big hat and you round up cattle and—' *Gulp.* 'And you live out in the middle of a prairie.'

'Yeah. I guess you could say I'm guilty of all that.'

Erin felt a swift surge of panic. Cowboys were *so* not her scene. She should get out of this fast. Now.

But she couldn't get past the absolute certainty that in every other way Luke felt so right for her, and he looked so incredibly delectable and at home right here, in the heart of Manhattan.

'If it helps, I promise not to yell out *yee-haa!* Or to call you ma'am or little lady,' he said with a clever switch to a Texan drawl.

He crossed his heart and his sexy grey eyes twinkled and she thought, What's the harm in having coffee?

'God, you're gorgeous.' Across a table in the diner Luke stared at her.

Erin pressed her hands to her cheeks to hide her blush, took a deep breath and then let it out quickly.

'Erin Reilly,' he said slowly, repeating her name as if he were tasting it, like vintage wine. 'With a name like that and with your colouring, you must have some Irish heritage.'

'My father's Irish. From County Clare.' She felt eerily excited, as bubbly as champagne, and the words just spilled out. 'But my mother's New York-Italian. My sister Angelina has dark hair and eyes, like our mom's side of the family.'

'And your father migrated here?'

'Yes, but then he went back to Ireland.'

Luke frowned. 'To stay?'

''Fraid so.'

'Without his family?'

To her surprise, she found that she wanted to explain it all, and she told this stranger more than she'd told many of her friends. 'Dad begged Mom to join him, but she won't leave Manhattan.'

Luke needed a moment or two to take this in. His grey eyes were pensive and then he seemed to shrug whatever bothered him aside. 'Have you been to Ireland to see your dad?' he asked.

'Yes, I've been over there quite a few times. I love Ireland.'

Luke seemed genuinely interested in everything about her and, because she felt so amazingly rapt yet relaxed, she found herself telling him a whole bunch of stuff about herself.

'And what about boyfriends?' he said.

'What about them?'

'Are you guys on this planet, or what?'

They both jumped as an impatient voice sounded close beside them.

'You ordered coffees, didn't you?' whined the waiter.

'Oh, yes, thanks.' They'd been so entranced with each other they hadn't even noticed him.

With a shake of his head, the waiter set their coffees down and bustled off muttering darkly about lovebirds.

Erin felt another blush hit her cheeks and Luke was grinning as he added sugar and cream to his coffee.

'You were about to tell me about your boyfriends,' he said after he'd tasted his coffee. 'Tell me the bad news. I know there must be an entire army of men beating a path to your door.'

She dropped her gaze and ran her finger over the handle of her coffee cup. 'No one special.'

Then, to cover her awkwardness, she demanded to hear all about Luke and his family.

He smiled. 'Actually, I'm a quarter Yank. My grandfather came from Louisiana.'

'Really? But he went to Australia?'

'Yeah. He was based in North Queensland during World War Two. At the end of the war, instead of asking my grandmother to travel to the US as a war bride, Grandad returned to Australia to work on our property, Warrapinya.'

'And he liked it? He stayed there?'

Luke nodded.

'Did it work out? Did your grandparents live happily ever after?' This question was suddenly very important to her.

He smiled. 'Couldn't be happier. I'd say their marriage was about as good as it gets.'

Luke told her more about his travels and about Australia and his cattle ranch, but then he looked around at the busy diner and said, 'This is so crowded in here. I haven't been to Central Park yet. Will you be my tour guide?'

Erin didn't hesitate. She showed him the way down Sixth Avenue and they strolled through the park beneath stately American elms and past cool green lawns until they reached the quiet serenity of Strawberry

Fields, and the whole time they walked they talked and they feasted their eyes on each other.

They didn't touch, not even to hold hands and yet their attraction was scorching. Exquisite. Erin couldn't be sure her feet were actually touching the ground.

Some time during that golden afternoon the fact that Luke was an Australian either became irrelevant or part of his allure— which, she could no longer be sure. Somewhere between the laughter and the longing, it simply didn't matter.

What mattered was the chemistry, the connection, the tug of honest-to-God lust and the promise of perfect friendship. What mattered was that she looked into his eyes and was filled with a wonderful sense of well-being, an intoxicating, inner radiance.

When they left Central Park through the West 72nd Street exit they couldn't bear to be parted. They dined together that evening. And afterwards, Erin asked Luke back to her apartment.

The outside world stopped for the next week.

By the end of it Erin was so heart-and-soul deep in love she couldn't imagine her life without Luke Manning.

'This week has been fabulous,' she told him.

He grinned. 'Only fabulous?'

She grinned back. 'Matchless then. Off the planet. The most wonderful seven days, surpassing anything I've ever dreamed of or hoped for.'

Drawing her close, he kissed her neck just below her left ear. 'You're perfect, Bright Eyes.'

'We're both amazing.'

'Olympic standard sex.'

'Gold-plated.'

He laughed. 'Damn right. We're the duck's pyjamas.'

But it wasn't just the love-making. They felt right in so many ways—they liked the same music, enjoyed the same movies, even laughed at the same moments in the movies. Erin loved to cook Thai and Luke loved to eat it.

'You mustn't leave me,' she said late one afternoon when they were sitting in the window-seat in her small living room. She paid more rent than she could sensibly afford for this tiny apartment, simply because she loved this seat in the window.

This was her private eyrie from which she watched her world. She loved sharing it with Luke. They sat opposite each other, legs entwined, drinking ginger tea out of over-sized bright violet cups and looking out across the city. Far below them neon signs flashed gaudy flickers into the twilight.

Luke sighed and avoided her gaze. 'There'll come a time soon when I'll have to go home. I have no choice. My parents are getting on in years and they rely on me to help run Warrapinya.'

'Well,' she said, after only the slightest pause, 'if you have absolutely no choice, I'll have to come with you.'

Luke couldn't hide his surprise. He put his cup down and reached for her hands. 'Erin, I couldn't ask you to do that.'

She pouted. 'Why? Don't you want me?'

'Of course I want you. I don't know how I'll survive without you.'

Yes. She could see the tummy-tumbling truth of it in his eyes.

'How do you plan to handle our relation-ship then? Do you have shares in an interna-tional airline?'

'I wish.'

His thumbs massaged the back of her hands.

'There's got to be a solution, Erin. But it wouldn't be fair to ask you to leave all this to come back to Australia. You'd hate to be stuck out in the bush where I live.'

'Your grandfather managed.'

'It was different for him.'

She looked at Luke and wondered how he could be so damnably calm while he talked about leaving her. Her insides were erupting. 'I wouldn't hate the bush if I was there with you, Luke. I'm sure I have a pioneering spirit. I could live on a ranch. When I was in primary school my favourite book was *Little House on the Prairie*.'

He made a light scoffing noise. 'The Outback's hot and dusty and lonely and isolated. You've spent your entire life in Manhattan, surrounded by people—by millions of people. The country around Warrapinya is empty. And it's dangerous.'

'Dangerous smangerous.' Setting aside her teacup, she pivoted forward, balancing on her knees till she was nose to nose with him. She smiled into his gorgeous grey eyes. 'The Outback's just wide open spaces and

gum trees and cows. It can't be more dangerous than the streets of Manhattan.'

He began to protest but she silenced him
with a long lush kiss on the mouth. 'Are
there muggers at Warrapinya?' she asked.

'There are deadly snakes and spiders, and
plenty of dirt and dust.'

'Dirt and dust?' Rolling her eyes to the
ceiling she gave a dismissive little laugh.
'You live in a proper house, don't you? With
a roof to keep the rain off and a bath to wash
the dirt off?'

'Yeah, but what about the isolation?'

She touched a fingertip to his divine lower
lip, traced its curve and watched desire warm
in his eyes. 'I'll have you there with me, Luke.'

'Minx.' Groaning softly, he drew her close
and wrapped his big arms around her and he
pressed kisses over her face and into the
white curve of her neck. But then, too soon,
he lifted his head and sighed again.

'What now?' she asked petulantly.

'What about your business?'

Oh, yes. Good question.

Erin suppressed a spiky surge of disquiet.
'Do you have a telephone and an Internet
connection?'

He shook his head. 'There are telephones, but no Internet.'

That stunned her.

'But the government assures us that we should all be connected over the next couple of years.'

Laughing a little wildly to cover her shock, she kissed the underside of his jaw. 'As long as I can have a table in a little corner somewhere, I can work, and if I can keep in touch with Angie by telephone and mail her the things I make, I can still operate my business. Everything should be fine.' She was so in love with him it was easy to believe in miracles.

Luke's hands gripped her shoulders and he set her a little apart from him. 'If you come with me, Erin, I want us to be married.'

'Do you?'

Marriage was an enormous step, but one look at the intense emotion in Luke's face and she knew that her question was foolish.

Well, if Luke wanted her as his wife, so be it. She wasn't letting him out of her sight.

But now, seven years later, here she was, sitting alone in a Sydney hotel, while her ex-husband and their son flew hundreds of miles north without her, and she told herself that Luke Manning might have said the words, but their decision to marry had been her fault.

She'd been the one who'd pleaded and cajoled. She'd known the power she held over him. She'd blocked his protests.

Blinded by her heart's yearnings, as careless as Eve, she'd led him to make the huge mistake of marrying her.

CHAPTER FIVE

'DAD's ranch is totally cool, Mom.'

'Oh, honey. How lovely to hear from you.'

Erin was sitting in a small pavement café eating breakfast—fresh melon and mango with yoghurt. Yesterday she'd checked her cellphone a thousand times. At least that was what it had felt like. She'd been desperate to hear from Joey but she'd been worried that Luke would consider her a fussy mother hen and so she'd held back from phoning.

'How are you?' she asked now.

'I'm great.'

'So you're having a good time?'

'Yep.'

'Was it fun in the plane yesterday?'

'You bet. Dad's an awesome pilot. An' he let me work one of the controls.'

'Holy sh—smoke.'

'I could see all the rivers and mountains and the roads and the rooftops and everything.' Joey giggled. 'An' guess what?'

'What?'

'I'm going to ride a horse this afternoon.'

'This afternoon?' Erin's heart took a dive, which was silly—she knew that sooner or later Luke would have his son on the back of a horse. 'Well…wow, Joey. That—that's neat. Are you scared?'

'Nah. Well…I might be a little scared.'

'Are you going to wear a helmet?'

'Um. I don't know. My horse is called Raven.'

'That's a pretty name, but Joey, you make sure you wear a helmet.'

'Raven's a mare, Mommy, and her coat is shiny and black. And guess what—Dad bought her just for me.'

'Goodness! A horse just for you? Aren't you lucky?'

But what about the helmet?

Erin knew she was overreacting but she couldn't help imagining the horror of her little city-bred boy falling from the back of a horse. She cringed as she pictured his head smashing into hard red dirt, his foot wrenched from a stirrup, his tiny body broken by trampling hooves. 'Joey, is Luke—is your father there?'

'Sure.'

'I—I'd like to speak to him, please.'

'Okay. Bye, Mommy.'

'You take care now. I love you, baby.'

'Erin?'

Luke's cool voice sent heat spiking through her.

'Oh, Luke, hi.'

'You want to speak to me?'

She gulped. 'Joey tells me he's going to start riding lessons today.'

'Yes. You got a problem with that?'

'I just wanted to—to—You are going to make sure he wears a helmet, aren't you?'

'Of course.'

Thank God. 'I'm sorry if I sound fussy, Luke, but Joey's still so little.'

'He's plenty old enough to start riding. The pony I'm putting him on has worked with children before. She's perfect. And I'll be watching the boy every minute he's on her back.'

'Yes... I'm sure you will.'

Luke sighed. 'I wish you would trust me with Joey.'

'I do trust you.'

'Forgive me for not noticing.' Lowering his voice, Luke said, 'If you jump on the phone every time you think up a new thing to worry about you're going to make the boy nervous.'

Erin gasped. Luke had virtually accused her of pestering him. How dared he? She'd restrained herself admirably last night and she hadn't initiated this call now.

'I don't need a lecture on how to communicate with my son.'

'Maybe not, but I'd appreciate it if you gave the boy space.' Luke's voice was calm yet merciless. 'I'd like him to have the chance to make up his own mind about me and my home and my lifestyle.'

'I'm giving him a chance. A big fat chance.' Erin's voice was choked with sudden fury. 'I'm giving him two whole months.'

And, because she couldn't stomach another smug response, she disconnected and snapped the cellphone shut before Luke could reply.

* * *

For three whole days there were no more phone calls between Sydney and Warrapinya. During that time Erin met Candia Hart, the diminutive, bubbly and super-successful Australian fashion designer. She visited art galleries and fashion houses, as well as jewellers, and she invested in some Australian gemstones. She particularly loved opals.

Then, to her surprise, Candia rang and invited her to dinner at her home. 'I'd love you to meet my husband, Andrea,' she said. 'Can you come on Saturday?'

Erin was elated. She hadn't really expected people as high profile as Candia and her famous racing-car driver husband, Andrea Conti, to be so friendly and hospitable.

Three nights later Joey called again.

'Are you having fun on the ranch?' she asked him.

'You shouldn't call this place a ranch, Mommy. It's a station. But there's no trains. Just humungous big trucks with carriages called dogs with hundreds and hundreds of cattle in them.'

'Sounds exciting. What have you been doing?'

'I've been to school.'

'Oh, come on, Joey, don't tell stories. I know that's not true. There aren't any schools at Warrapinya.'

'There's a school here, Mommy. I did home school with Brad and Clint and Jason. Over the Internet. It's totally cool.'

'Who are Brad and Clint and Jason?'

'They're my cousins.'

She heard the deep rumble of Luke's voice in the background.

'They're my second cousins,' Joey corrected. 'And they're so cool, Mommy. You should see how good they are at horse-riding.'

The wistful note of admiration in his voice sparked a twinge of anxiety in Erin. Joey's sheltered ultra-urban life in Manhattan, where trips to Central Park provided the only encounters with nature, must seem terribly tame compared with this wonderful outdoor adventure.

'They do barrel racing and calf riding,' Joey said. 'But Dad won't let me.'

Feeling faint, Erin asked, 'How—how old

are these boys?' Was Joey mixing with teen-agers?

'Brad's eight and Clint's seven, I think. Jason's only five.'

'Five?' Somehow she managed not to shriek. But good grief, if she'd known there would be little boys Joey's age performing outrageous hair-raising rodeo stunts she would have…she would have…

What? Insisted on accompanying Joey to Warrapinya? No, of course not. That wasn't feasible. She didn't want to go there and Luke would resent her presence. He and Joey needed space.

Remembering that and Luke's warning that she mustn't make Joey worried, she finished the conversation rather quickly, keeping her farewell brief and upbeat.

Erin's anxiety about Joey lingered. On Saturday, when she was preparing to go to Candia and Andrea's for dinner, she felt more uneasy than ever. She decided that she really must make a call to Warrapinya to put her mind at rest. Only then would she be able to relax and be a pleasant dinner guest.

A woman's voice answered. 'Oh, hello,

Erin. We haven't met, but I'm Jenny, Luke's cousin.'

'You must be the mother of the famous Brad and Clint and Jason?'

'Yes. I'm afraid so.' Jenny seemed surprisingly apologetic. 'I'm so sorry the boys set your son a bad example.'

'What do you mean? What example was that?'

On the other end of the line there was a soft sound, somewhere between a groan and a sigh. It sounded almost guilty. 'You haven't heard from Luke?'

'No.' Fighting panic, Erin closed her eyes and her hand gripped the receiver so hard her fingers hurt. 'What's happened? Can I speak to Joey?'

'No, I'm afraid you can't. He's not here.'

Oh, God. Erin felt as if she'd been dangled over the edge of a very high precipice.

'There's been an accident,' Jenny said. 'Luke's flown Joey in to the hospital in Townsville.'

CHAPTER SIX

LUKE stood at the far end of the long hospital corridor, his hands weighted deep in his pockets.

Staring through a tall narrow window into the black night, he let his mind replay again and again his feelings of terror when he'd heard a cry for help and had rushed to the horse yard to find Raven prancing nervously and Joey lying unconscious in the dirt.

Could there be a worse moment for a father? Gut-wrenching didn't go halfway to describing how he'd felt as he'd scooped Joey's tiny limp body into his arms. He'd been filled with the darkest dread. Absolutely terrified. Appalled.

Luke couldn't remember how he'd got Joey to the plane. The frantic call he'd put through to the hospital and the take-off from

Warrapinya were a blur. All he could remember was the agonising impact of his love for his boy exploding through him like a grenade. Joey was such a smart, cute, loving little kid. He was his son. Oh, God, how could he have let this happen to his own son?

His anger had surfaced later. Much later. It stirred him again now. This accident should not have happened. It wouldn't have happened if Joey hadn't disobeyed him. But a father couldn't be expected to watch his boy every second. He should have been able to trust Joey to do as he was told.

Maybe the kid lacked discipline. Perhaps Erin had been too soft with him.

At the thought of Erin Luke's gut dropped. Hell, she'd be a mess when she heard about this. She'd be so mad at him. She might never forgive him.

Just the same, he should try to ring her again. Grimacing at the thought, he reached into his pocket for his mobile phone and in the same instant he glanced to the far end of the corridor just as the lift doors opened and someone emerged.

* * *

Erin saw Luke as soon as she stepped out of the elevator. She saw the hunch of his shoulders.

Oh, God. Joey…

Luke looked so desolate her heart clattered like a metal pan dropped by a careless nurse.

Then Luke turned and saw her and he stiffened, his shoulders shooting back in surprise. Or maybe anger. It was too bad if he was mad at her intrusion. She'd had to come.

He began to hurry down the shiny linoleum towards her and her heart pounded. Soon she would know the worst. He would tell her what had happened to her baby.

The grimness of his expression made her break into a run. 'Where's Joey?' she cried and then her legs gave way and she stumbled.

Luke caught her, gripped her by the elbows and steadied her.

Terrified, she lifted her gaze to meet his and she forced herself to repeat her dreadful question. 'Where's Joey? How— how is he?'

Luke's face was pale beneath his tan, his

eyes storm-dark. She pressed a hand against the awful crashing in her chest.

'Joey's okay,' Luke said. 'He's here in this ward. He's asleep.'

'But he's really okay?'

'Yes. He's going to be fine.'

'Oh.'

She'd been so tense, so prepared to hear bad news that her knees gave way completely. She sagged into Luke, her head falling on to his shoulder, her heart beating frantically against his upper arm.

She was forced to cling to him, shaking, tearful, exhausted, her fingers curling, grasping at the fabric of his sweater. Without the support of his arms she would have slid to the floor.

'Are you sure?' she whispered. It seemed too good to be true and she was terrified that she'd misheard him.

'Yes, Erin. Joey's fine. He regained consciousness on the flight in, but the doctors gave him a CT scan just to make certain there's no serious injury. They're confident he's fine—just a little concussed—so he has to stay here for twenty-four hours, but that's simply a precaution.'

'Thank God. I've been so worried.'

Joey's okay. Joey isn't going to die. He isn't maimed. He's fine.

She let her mind replay those beautiful words, repeating them over and over, until their true meaning sank in and the fearful terror began to loosen its icy hold. Finally she felt a lift in her heart, the first warm ripple of relief.

Only then did she take in other details. Good grief. She was in Luke's arms. She was *plastered* against him. Luke's lips were brushing her forehead. His hand was gently cradling her head against his bulky shoulder. She could feel his heartbeats and the warmth of his hand as he stroked her hair.

She was even aware of his smell—a mixture of sunlit pastures and dusty man. It was achingly familiar. And everything about the fit of their bodies felt familiar too, so wonderfully right. Reassuring. His fingers were so gentle as he stroked the hair at her nape.

But what was Luke thinking? What was he feeling? Did he really want to hold her, or was he doing it out of a sense of duty? Or guilt?

Perhaps he was simply calming her the way he might calm a frightened animal.

Or perhaps he was remembering all the times he'd held her in the past….

From behind them came the rumble of a trolley being pushed down the corridor. Sanity returned. Erin lifted her head from Luke's shoulder.

She gave him a little nudge with her elbow and he let her go quickly, swinging his arms open and then down to his sides while she made a business of rescuing her pashmina from the floor, but when she wrapped it around her once more she still felt cold and she would have liked the comfort of Luke's arms.

But there were limits to how much a divorced couple could share. The sob-fest was over. Luke had seen her at her worst, at her most vulnerable and helpless, but it was time to be strong again, to stand on her own two feet.

And it was time to remember that she was actually angry with this man.

'Why didn't you call me to tell me about Joey?' She snapped this question even more sharply than she'd meant to.

Luke's sudden smile surprised her. 'That's more like it,' he said. 'I knew you'd have to lash out at me sooner or later.'

Erin gasped. Is that what Luke expected? Was she so predictable? But then she remembered that she had every right to be angry with this man.

'Don't sidestep, Luke. Surely I deserved a phone call?'

He released a weary sigh. 'It was an emergency, Erin. Joey was my first priority. The only phone calls I had time for were to the hospital.'

'But after that? You must have known how worried I'd be?'

'I tried to ring you when the main drama was over. Actually, I've been trying to call you for the past couple of hours.'

Her shoulders lifted in a defensive little shrug. 'I've been on the plane. I couldn't use my cellphone.'

She chewed at her lower lip in a vexed kind of way and was disturbed to see Luke watching her. He was watching her mouth, to be exact, watching it intensely and in a way that sent her insides into meltdown.

'Anyway,' she said even more snappily.

'How did this accident happen? How could Joey fall from a horse? I thought you were supposed to be supervising his every moment while he was on the thing. You promised me he'd wear a helmet.'

Instead of answering her, Luke placed a firm hand at her elbow and steered her closer to the window. Erin almost jerked her arm away from him. But then she felt foolish when she realised he was guiding her out of the way of a nurse wheeling a trolley of medicines. Heavens, she was as tense as a trip-wire.

'I wasn't there when it happened, because Joey disobeyed me,' Luke said. 'He was mad at me because I wouldn't let him try barrel racing with the other boys.'

'Barrel racing? I can't believe any responsible parent would let little boys do anything so dangerous.'

'It's not dangerous for Outback kids. For them, riding a horse and trying a few rodeo stunts is no more of a risk than riding a bike or a skateboard and throwing a few wheelies for a city kid.'

'Not for this city kid. You don't know the first thing about Joey, Luke. At home, if he wants to ride his bike, I personally go with him and supervise him in the park.'

'He must enjoy that,' Luke said with a cynical roll of his eyes.

Erin ground her teeth. Had this journey to Australia been a mistake? Had she been mad to turn her little boy loose in the wilds of the Outback? She should have asked Luke to come to New York. Or they should have met on neutral ground—in California or even Hawaii—or—

She stopped in mid-thought. 'Did you say Joey disobeyed you?'

Luke nodded.

'How? What happened?'

'Jenny's boys were kept busy indoors today, catching up on schoolwork they missed. I was doing paperwork in my office and Joey was supposed to be playing a video game in the lounge room, but the little devil snuck out. He took Raven down to the paddock behind the stables and tried to practise barrel racing—bareback—on his own.'

'Bareback?' Erin gaped at him. 'Good grief, Luke, how on earth could a little boy Joey's size get up on to a bareback horse?'

'He climbed a fence and jumped on—because he didn't know how to saddle her.' Erin was sure she caught a flash of pride in Luke's eyes. 'He must have figured it was his only option.'

She was stunned. 'I can't believe that Joey would even *think* that he could ride bareback.' She couldn't imagine her little boy trying anything so reckless, so daring. The poor kid must have been desperate to be like the other boys.

She closed her eyes. Joey was out of his depth in the Outback—just as she had been.

Some of the station hands at Warrapinya had called her 'the boss's Manhattan mistake.' She'd overheard them. It had hurt terribly at the time, but she knew they were right. She hadn't been cut out for the life there.

And neither was Joey.

Poor Joey. He hadn't asked to be born into this mess.

She took a deep breath and turned to Luke again, and she saw for the first time how tired and strained he looked. 'I guess you must have had a terrible shock too,' she admitted.

He nodded slowly and swallowed. Without looking at her, he said, 'The boy means the world to me, Erin.'

Then he flicked a wary gaze her way and she caught a glimpse of deep emotion in his eyes—a mixture of sorrow and love and longing—and her heart seemed to swell so hugely in her chest she couldn't speak.

She wanted to tell Luke that she understood his pain. She cared. She almost wanted to tell him how much she'd missed him, how many times in the past five years she'd regretted leaving him.

But how foolish was that? She had no idea if he'd welcome such news.

They stood uncomfortably, not looking at each other and not talking.

Finally Luke said, 'Would you like to see Joey now?'

'Yes—yes, please.'

'He's probably still asleep.'

'That's okay.'

They walked together down the corridor till Luke stopped outside a door that was slightly ajar. Erin glimpsed a night-light on the wall and the corner of a hospital bed, neat with stiff white sheets, perfectly tucked.

Even though she knew Joey was okay, she felt a pang of anxiety. Her poor baby was all alone in a strange big hospital.

As if he sensed how she felt, Luke sent her a faint smile and a reassuring wink that did ridiculous things to her heart, and then he pushed the door open.

Joey looked so small in the middle of the white bed and there was an ugly graze and a bump on his forehead. Erin tiptoed forward and his eyes opened slowly and he smiled just a little groggily.

'Mommy,' he said softly. His eyes seemed to study her and then he frowned. 'What are you doing here?'

'I came straight from Sydney when I heard about your fall,' she said, leaning over to kiss his cheek. 'How are you, baby? Do I get a hug?'

'Sure.' Sleepily, he lifted his arms to her. 'You smell nice,' he said as she hugged him. 'Doesn't Mommy smell nice, Dad?'

Behind her Luke cleared his throat. 'Very,' he murmured so quietly Erin almost missed it.

Joey's eyes became worried. 'I'm sorry, Mommy. I forgot my skid lid.'

'Your what?'

'His skull cap,' said Luke.

'Oh, yes.' Tenderly, Erin touched the side of Joey's head near the bump. 'You've learned the hard way why those helmets are important, haven't you?'

Joey nodded and then winced as if the movement hurt his head.

'I've just popped in to say goodnight,' Erin told him. 'You look as if you need a nice long sleep.'

'Are you going to stay here with me?'

Before Erin could respond, Luke moved closer to the bed. 'We'll wait with you now until you go to sleep and then we'll see you again first thing in the morning.' He spoke gently, but with an unmistakable air of fatherly authority that took Erin by surprise.

The three of them chatted a little about the hospital and whether Joey's head hurt, whether the nurses were nice and what he'd had for dinner. Fifteen minutes later, Joey was asleep again.

Outside his room, Erin turned to Luke. 'I'd like to speak to a nurse. I thought Joey seemed too lethargic, didn't you?'

'I spoke to the sister in charge earlier and

she said concussion often makes the patient sleepy, even a little confused. I wouldn't worry, Erin. He's in expert hands and he should be much better tomorrow. Come on, let's go. Have you had dinner?'

Erin dismissed dinner with a wave of her hand. 'Before we head off, we should talk about what's going to happen tomorrow, when Joey gets out of hospital.'

Luke frowned. 'I don't catch your drift.'

'Is there somewhere nearby where I can take him?'

'I'll take him home.'

'No. Joey can't go back to Warrapinya, Luke.'

'Why the hell not?'

'Ssh.' She cast a hasty glance back through the doorway to Joey's darkened room and lowered her voice to just above a whisper. 'He won't be well enough to go back out there.'

'He's only had a bump on the head. He's going to be fine in a day or two.'

'But once he gets back there, he'll be tearing around with those wild little boys again and he'll want to go horse-riding.'

'I'll make sure he takes it easy till he's completely recovered.'

Erin felt her jaw clench. Anger stirred. Luke didn't understand how unprepared Joey was for the Outback. And he couldn't imagine how hard it was for her to let her little boy go off into the wilderness again. It had been hard enough the first time, but now, after a potentially fatal accident— 'You don't understand what he means to me,' she said.

'Maybe you don't understand what he means to me.'

Blue eyes and grey glared at each other.

Then Erin dropped her gaze and sighed. Actually, she did understand how Luke felt. But he was asking too much of her.

'I'm his mother,' she said. 'Joey will need me.'

He would need her now the way he'd needed her so many times—when he had the chicken pox, or when he woke in the night from a bad dream, or when he was scared that aliens might abduct him.

Luke's brows drew low over narrowed eyes. 'You can't cut off my time with Joey like that. I won't stand for it. The deal was two months.'

'The deal was you'd take good care of him.'

'That's below the belt, Erin, and you know it.'

She closed her eyes to avoid the menace in Luke's. Well, yes, perhaps she had over-reacted. Again.

And she also knew that Joey adored Luke. If she tried to stop him from going back with his father, how would the boy react?

Luke began to march with angry strides down the corridor to the lift and Erin hurried to keep up. Was she being churlish because deep down she was afraid? Was she jealous because she knew that Luke could give Joey the comfort and love that had been her exclusive role till now?

It wasn't pleasant to realise that she was handling this badly. She'd been hoping she would learn something from these two months of separation, that she would grow stronger emotionally, even that she would emerge from this ordeal a better person.

'I'm sorry,' she said, as they came to a halt in front of the elevator. 'You're right, Luke,' she added bravely. 'I'm probably overreact-ing. I'll have to trust you to take good care of Joey. If the doctor gives him the all-clear he should go back with you.'

'Thanks,' he said gruffly. 'That means a lot.'

On the ground floor they crossed the hospital foyer and approached a wall of floor-to-ceiling glass doors. Beyond the glass the car park loomed and for the first time since she'd grabbed a taxi in Sydney and dashed to Mascot airport, Erin thought about what would happen next. She'd flown north in a blind panic with no more than overnight clothes and a tooth-brush, and now it was time to get practical.

'This is the way to the cab rank,' Luke said, indicating a door to their left.

'Have you organised your accommodation?'

'Sure.' He smiled. 'Last year I bought an apartment here in Townsville.'

'You bought a condo, here on the coast?'

'That's right. It's handy for trips into the city.'

'I'll bet it is.' It was hard to hide her shock. Once again Erin was conscious of how much more comfortable Luke's life was now.

There'd been no plane for emergencies and no regular trips to town when they had been married. She'd spent her days stuck out in the middle of the wilderness, lonely and scared, while Luke had been off mustering cattle or mending fences or doing a thousand other things that had kept him away from the homestead.

'I have a spare bed,' Luke said. 'You're welcome to it.'

'I—I don't think that's wise,' she stammered, surprised that he would offer her hospitality.

Luke stopped walking and there was a hint of mild amusement lurking in his eyes, almost as if he were challenging her. 'Why the hell isn't it wise?'

'Because...of our situation.'

His hands settled on his hips and his mouth curled into a faintly contemptuous sneer. 'You're scared of me.'

Yes, she was scared—scared of the effect he had on her—of the way her body had gone into meltdown when he'd held her. Scared of his body's answering response.

She remembered Angie's question about sparks. Oh, yes, there were sparks all right. Electrifying, dangerous sparks.

But what she had to remember was that this trip to Australia wasn't about her falling in lust again with Luke. Giving in to physical hunger would be the worst kind of mistake. It couldn't lead to anything but more confusion and unhappiness for everyone concerned, especially for Joey.

'Of course I'm not scared of you,' she said carefully. 'It's just that I—I don't want to impose on you. A bed for the night is a very kind offer, but there's no need. I can find a room somewhere.'

'It would be less of an imposition if you could get rid of that bee in your bonnet and be sensible, Erin. Why not stay at my place? The spare room's there to be used. Have you realised how late it is? Do you really want the hassle of trying to track down a motel room at this time of night?'

He was right, of course, but his taunting reasonableness annoyed her. Why wasn't he as uptight as she was about the two of them spending a night together in his apartment, under his roof, behind a locked door and within the privacy of his four walls?

But, given his coolness, her nervous objections appeared childish. Her hands fluttered away from her sides, palms up, signalling her surrender. 'Okay, thank you, Luke. A bed at your place would be very…convenient.'

A taxi took them across Ross River and into the city and they sat carefully apart on the back seat. Erin couldn't believe how nervous she felt. Her skin seemed to hum all over with heightened awareness of Luke's proximity.

What was the matter with her? He was her ex, the one man in the world she'd tried to live with and couldn't. And yet here she was with the kind of tummy-twisting anticipation she hadn't felt since her high school prom night.

She looked out at the street lights and the traffic and the lights shining from suburban houses—high set timber homes mostly, surrounded by tree-filled gardens—and she found herself remembering a time when they were married when Luke had promised to bring her here to Townsville.

'I want to take you and the little fellow and we'll have a holiday in Townsville,' he'd said. 'You'll love it. We can rent a cottage on Magnetic Island or an apartment in the city and we'll hire a babysitter and go out. There's a Shakespeare play on.'

She'd been incredibly excited. The promise of that little trip to town had kept her

GET FREE BOOKS and a FREE MYSTERY GIFT WHEN YOU PLAY THE...

Just scratch off the silver box with a coin. Then check below to see the gifts you get!

SLOT MACHINE GAME!

YES! I have scratched off the silver box. Please send me the four FREE books and mystery gift for which I qualify. I understand I am under no obligation to purchase any books, as explained on the back of this card. I am over 18 years of age.

N6EI

Mrs/Miss/Ms/Mr _____ Initials _____

BLOCK CAPITALS PLEASE

Surname _____

Address _____

_____

Postcode _____

Worth FOUR FREE BOOKS plus a BONUS Mystery Gift!

Worth FOUR FREE BOOKS!

Worth ONE FREE BOOK!

TRY AGAIN!

Visit us online at www.millsandboon.co.uk

The Reader Service™ — Here's how it works:

Accepting the free books places you under no obligation to buy anything. You may keep the books and gift and return the despatch note marked 'cancel'. If we do not hear from you, about a month later we'll send you 6 brand new books and invoice you just £2.80* each. That's the complete price - there is no extra charge for postage and packing. You may canc at any time, otherwise every month we'll send you 6 more books, which you may either purchase or return to us - the choice is yours.

*Terms and prices subject to change without notice.

THE READER SERVICE™
FREE BOOK OFFER
FREEPOST CN81
CROYDON
CR9 3WZ

NO STAMP
NECESSARY
IF POSTED IN
THE U.K. OR N.I.

buoyed for days, but then at the last minute they couldn't go. There'd been a problem on a neighbouring property and Luke had claimed that he couldn't abandon these people. They were good neighbours and the Manning family owed them a big favour.

Erin had been devastated. Surely Luke owed her a favour too?

And then the wet season had arrived early and they had been cut off from the coast by flooded creeks. Without a plane they'd been stranded.

They hadn't had their holiday. By the time the wet season had been over it had been time to check fences and to shift the cattle again.

The taxi pulled up at a tall apartment block right in the heart of the city. Erin noticed a trendy-looking sushi bar on the ground floor and a hairdresser and a beauty spa right across the street. Luke's apartment was on the top floor and it was spacious and very modern and new, with stunning views across the southern suburban lights to the silky waters of the bay.

She looked around her in amazement. She was pleased for Luke that he was enjoying such luxuries, but she couldn't help feeling a little angry too. She felt as if she'd been cheated somehow.

So much had happened in the past five years. She'd struggled alone to make a success of her business and to care for Joey, while Luke had gone from strength to strength. He'd acquired a manager who'd brought his young family to live at Warrapinya, and he had an aeroplane and this apartment.

The spare room Luke showed her to was very trendy and comfortable and, she was relieved to see, separated from the master bedroom by a spacious open-plan living area.

'I'm going to order some take-away,' Luke said. 'Do you still like Thai? They have a great Thai restaurant just down the street.'

'Thai sounds great.'

He looked down at his clothes. He'd probably dropped everything when Joey's accident occurred and he was still wearing his working gear—dusty jeans and riding boots and a rough denim work-shirt beneath a faded and holey navy cotton sweater.

By contrast, Erin was dressed for dinner

in a cream silk shirt and caramel silk trousers.

'I'm going to get out of these and take a shower,' Luke said. 'If you want one, your bathroom's that way. You should find a bathrobe in there.' Eyeing her tiny overnight bag, he flashed a slightly self-conscious boyish grin. 'I can't offer you much in the way of clothes, except the bathrobe or one of my shirts.'

'The robe will be fine,' she said tightly, but she wasn't going to get changed into it yet. She would keep all her clothes on, thank you.

While Luke showered she went through to the bathroom and washed her face, cleaned her teeth and tidied her hair. There was a big mirror above the vanity table and she studied her reflection. Her clothes had seemed so right for a dinner party at Candia's home in Potts Point, Sydney, but now she was with Luke they felt totally wrong. It was as if she was trying too hard.

She looked at the strands of freshwater pearls on fine gold chains about her neck. Her earrings were little balls she'd made from twisted gold wire and seed pearls. She

loved her jewellery, but now it seemed un-
necessary and she slipped off the chains and
removed the baubles from her ears.

Kicking off her Prada pumps, she
wandered back into the living room,
thought about coffee and continued on to
the kitchen.

'That coffee smells great,' Luke said
when he emerged, freshly showered and
changed into clean jeans and a spotless
white T-shirt that hugged his physique with
breathtaking snugness. 'I'm glad you've
made yourself at home.'

His eyes held hers for a moment longer
than was necessary. 'You've taken off those
dangly things.'

'So?'

'It's a pity. I liked them.'

Heat flared in her cheeks and she quickly
switched her attention to the coffee-maker.
It was time to put an end to this nonsense,
to dampen the undeniable sizzle.

'Would you like some of this coffee?' she
asked.

'I think I'll grab a beer.' He opened the
fridge and freed a can from a six-pack.
'Make yourself at home.' He cocked his head

towards the living room. 'Dinner should be here in about fifteen minutes.'

The sofas in the living room were deep and comfortable, and Erin curled into one corner and tucked her legs beneath her, determined to be casual and relaxed.

'Don't look so worried, Erin.'

So much for looking casual and relaxed. She smiled ruefully. 'You have to admit it's kind of weird, Luke, being together like this after such a long time.'

'Yeah.' He took a swig of beer, lowered it and stared at the floor for so long he had time to count all the stripes on the black and sienna rug.

Erin looked at her hands folded neatly in her lap. Each nail was perfectly shaped and immaculately painted. She found herself thinking of the unpainted, no-nonsense hands of the women in the Outback—hands that could handle heavy gear shifts as they steered a truck across a dry creek gully—hands that baked bread, delivered breech calves and helped their husbands to build stockyards.

Luke's voice broke into her thoughts. 'I guess this is a chance for us to talk.'

She reached for her mug and took a deep

sip of coffee. 'Well, yes, I guess it is. Why don't you tell me more about how you and Joey are getting along?'

'We're hitting it off just fine. He's a terrific little bloke. I must admit I didn't expect to get on so well so quickly.'

'I told you in Sydney, you're his hero.'

'Yes.' He sent her a perplexed smile and scratched his head. 'I just don't understand how it happened. How can I be the kid's hero when I haven't been around? He couldn't have known the first thing about me.'

'That's the point, Luke,' Erin said gently. 'I'm afraid an absent father leaves rather a big hole in a little boy's life and he fills it the best way he can.'

Luke's face darkened as he shifted uncomfortably. His eyes flashed with concern.

Erin took a deep breath. She could never think about Luke and Joey together without also feeling guilty for separating them. But the fault hadn't all been hers. Luke had remained obstinately remote and silent. He hadn't tried to see Joey.

Perhaps it was time to come clean, to explain to Luke exactly why she'd brought his son to Australia.

'Joey really needed to meet you, Luke. He was a boy on the edge.'

'Edge of what?'

'Disaster.'

CHAPTER SEVEN

'YOU'VE got to be joking,' Luke cried. 'How could a happy little bloke like Joey be heading for disaster?'

Erin bristled. 'Why do you think I suddenly wrote to you and asked if he could meet you?'

'I—I just thought—' Luke broke off and he felt suddenly lost as he stared at her. Eventually he forced a weak smile. 'I suppose I thought you'd suddenly realised how desperate I was to meet my son.'

Now, he realised, he'd given Erin the perfect opportunity to demand why he hadn't done something about that. Why, after their divorce, had he refused any further contact with her? Why had he made no attempt to contact Joey?

But perhaps she was wise enough to know

that these questions would only lead to more tension. They would never be able to talk this through if they got too tense.

'I'm afraid your feelings weren't my first priority, Luke,' she said quietly. 'I was only thinking of Joey. You see, I've been very worried about him ever since he started school last fall.'

'What happened?'

'I guess mixing with so many other kids brought the whole father issue to the surface.' She swallowed nervously and fiddled with the handle of her coffee cup. 'Until then I hadn't talked to Joey about you.'

'Never?'

'No. I'm sorry. I know it sounds terrible. And now I look back I can see it was a mistake. A big mistake. But until then Joey didn't ask questions about you and you didn't seem to want to have anything to do with us, and the whole subject was rather painful for me, so—' Erin paused and cleared her throat. 'For a lot of reasons I found it easier just to pretend you didn't exist.'

Luke swallowed to try to shift the painful rock wedged in his throat.

'Soon after Joey started school, I realised that I'd created a bigger problem by never talking about you,' she said. 'Joey's a bright, sensitive little boy and he'd picked up that in our house the Daddy topic was scary.'

She sent him a quick, anxious glance.

'You were on the other side of the world, Luke. I didn't know what to do.'

He knew she expected a response from him, but he couldn't speak. The rock was still there in his throat. He was picturing her, alone in Manhattan, with Joey and without him, Joey's father.

She looked so vulnerable as she sat there telling him this—vulnerable, yet gorgeous with her blue eyes shimmering with the hint of tears and her lovely silken clothes clinging to her in all the right places.

Why the hell had he been such a stubborn bastard? Why hadn't he chased after her when she'd left? It didn't make sense any more that he'd gone to so much trouble to shut down his emotions, to have nothing to do with her.

What had he achieved besides leaving his son totally confused? Erin was right, it was a bloody disaster.

Erin, realising he wasn't going to comment, continued. 'Joey compensated by inventing elaborate fantasies about you,' she said. 'I guess they reassured him, but they scared the hell out of me.'

'What kind of fantasies?'

'Oh, he'd tell people that you were a soldier fighting overseas, or that you lived at the North Pole with Santa Claus. He told my mother that you lived in a satellite in outer space. And my sister heard him telling her neighbours that you had a hotdog stand on a New York street corner and you gave away free treats to children.'

'I was a pretty cool guy.' Luke tried for humour and missed. 'Hell, Erin, what did you do?'

'At first I thought it would be easy to fix. I tried to set everything straight by digging out a photo of you. I found one of you on a stock horse at Warrapinya, looking like a cowboy out of a western movie, and Joey was thrilled. But—' She sighed heavily. 'Unfortunately the photo triggered the whole hero thing and Joey just got more and more obsessed with you.'

He could imagine how much it must have

hurt Erin to tell him this. She'd poured so much love into raising her little son, and then the boy had turned around and started hero-worshipping a vague image of a cattleman on the other side of the world.

'I had to ask myself how healthy it can be for a little boy to be infatuated with a photo,' she said.

Luke stared at the toe of his boot. 'There must be stacks of kids who don't know their father.'

'Well, yes, that's what I told myself, but just the same I couldn't stop worrying, so I decided to have a chat with Joey's teacher. She said she'd been about to phone me because she was concerned too. Apparently, all Joey talked about at school was you. He drew countless pictures of you. You were the subject of just about every "show and tell" session. She said the other kids knew he was making it all up and they'd begun to tease him.'

Luke swore softly.

'She suggested I speak to a child psychologist.'

'I can't believe this.' Luke picked up his beer and set it down again.

'The psychologist was very good,' Erin said. 'He helped me to understand that the way a boy views his father becomes a part of how he views himself. Joey's self-esteem is tied up in his image of you. If he's mixed up and confused, or if he becomes overly anxious about his father's identity, his chances for long-term happiness are at stake.'

'God, Erin.'

'I was shocked to realise that I was letting Joey down,' she said, her voice faltering now with her effort to hold her own tears at bay. 'I made myself sick with worry.' Her jaw tightened as if she was struggling for control. 'I'd failed as a wife, but I was desperate to be a good mom. I'd always thought that being Joey's mommy was the best thing I've done. But suddenly I was scared that I'd failed as a mother too.'

In the distance the intercom buzzer rang.

Erin glanced at Luke, expecting him to answer it, but he was sitting very still, staring at her, his eyes so bleak they were chips of grey slate.

After several seconds of silence, he reached across the table and covered her hand with his. 'You haven't failed at all. You're a fabulous mother, Erin. Joey's a great little guy, a real credit to you.'

His touch sent sparks tingling over her skin, sparks that kept going, all the way through her.

The buzzer sounded again.

'Isn't that our dinner?' she asked, not sure whether she was relieved or dismayed by the interruption.

Luke frowned and then blinked. 'Oh, yes, I guess it must be.' He jumped to his feet. 'Excuse me.' He headed for the door, returning quickly with clear plastic containers.

Erin hurried to the kitchen and found blue and white Asian-style bowls, woven straw mats and cutlery. The interruption was timely, she realised as she set these things on the glass-topped table in the dining nook.

She and Luke had been getting too close when they talked about Joey. But she'd done what was required, she'd set Luke straight about his son. Now it was time to step back a little.

'This food smells amazing,' she said as Luke removed the lids from containers of jasmine rice, chicken curry and garlic and pepper chicken. 'I've just realised I'm starving. I gave up a special dinner invitation to fly here tonight.'

'A date?'

It was tempting to let him think so, but as they sat opposite each other, scooping rice and chicken into their bowls, she told him about the dinner invitation to Candia and Andrea's.

'You're moving into the social stratosphere,' he said.

'Not really. It's more like I'm indulging in a little shameless name-dropping.'

They were both hungry and eating became their focus. 'This is delicious,' she said.

'Thanks for explaining about Joey,' Luke said after a bit and then he released a heavy sigh and set down his fork. 'I love him, Erin. I really do.'

She nodded, not quite sure what else to say.

'There was a time after you left me when I completely lost it, and I actually thought about legally contesting my right to Joey.'

A piece of chicken seemed to stick in her throat. She swallowed with difficulty.

'I went through a stage where I could

totally relate to those crazy blokes who abduct their own kids.'

'Oh, God, Luke, I'm so glad you didn't do anything like that.'

She made the mistake of looking at him. His face was contorted as if he were battling deep and painful emotion. She couldn't bear it. She wanted to cry.

'But I knew I was only going to inflict more pain on you,' he said. 'That was how I justified making a total break from you both.'

Oh, Luke, if only you hadn't...

After so many years of silence it was too much. To Erin's dismay, her face crumpled suddenly. She pressed a hand over her mouth, willing herself to get a grip. Luke was breaking her heart but she couldn't fall apart now.

If only you hadn't cut yourself off. If only you'd come after me...

She couldn't look at him. She drew a shaky deep breath and then another. It was too late to tell Luke how naïve and immature she'd been five years ago—that when she'd left she'd hoped he'd come racing after her to tell her that his love for her and for Joey was greater than his feelings for Warrapinya.

Such silly, *silly* dreams...

She shouldn't be remembering them now. She should only be thinking about Joey, about what was best for his future. Her feelings for his father weren't the issue.

How selfish she was.

She wasn't sure how long she sat staring at the bowl in front of her, thinking how easy it would be now, as she sat here talking to Luke, to make the same foolish mistakes all over again.

But she doubted that Luke was thinking such thoughts. He was helping himself to more food and he cast a cautious smile her way. 'Joey told me you broke up with your boyfriend, some opera singer guy.'

Her sigh was accompanied by an embarrassed roll of her eyes. 'Thank you, Joey.' She lifted her chin. 'Sebastian wasn't a big deal. I wasn't cut up about him.'

'Joey told me that too.'

'Oh? Did you interrogate Joey about my boyfriends?'

Luke's expression was impassive. 'He volunteered the information...but yes, I was interested.'

'But my dates aren't really any of your business,' she felt compelled to insist. 'I have no intention of asking you about the women in your life.'

He smiled enigmatically. 'Aren't you just a little curious?'

'Not in the least.'

Liar. Erin hated how uptight and prim she sounded. She glanced very deliberately at her watch and yawned. 'I hadn't realised how late it is.'

'You can do better than that, Erin.'

'Than what?'

He chuckled. 'That was a very theatrical yawn. Anyway, you can't go to bed; you haven't tried the seafood yet. Besides, my list of women friends isn't so long that it should scare you away.'

'That's hardly the point.' She was getting annoyed with him. Really annoyed.

With exaggerated concentration she spooned seafood and vegetables into her bowl. 'Why on earth do you think I'd be interested in your sex life?'

He didn't answer, but he watched the way her hand shook as she tried to spear a piece of broccoli and his knowing smile made her want to throw down the fork dramatically, leap from her chair and flounce out of the room.

The problem was, she knew that her anger was sparked by an urgent need to cover the wave of wild, totally irrational jealousy that swept through her when Luke mentioned his girlfriends.

She forced herself to stay there till she'd finished the food, but then she quickly pushed the bowl from her. 'Thanks, that was delicious, but if you'll excuse me I think I'll go straight to bed.'

A teasing glint silvered Luke's eyes. 'What about a nightcap? I'm planning to sit on the balcony for a bit and watch the moon. Why don't you join me?'

'No, thank you.'

'We could talk about—'

'We've done enough talking. You sit out there and enjoy the moon and your drink, Luke. And while you're there, you might like to think about how often you would like to see Joey in the future.'

Her shot found its mark. The sudden chill in Luke's eyes was angry enough to ensure Erin spent another restless night.

Next morning Luke was withdrawn and pre-occupied so they didn't speak much. Erin told herself that she didn't mind. Last night, when they'd talked about Joey, she'd felt as if she and Luke had been building a very fragile bridge. But then he'd spoiled it by reminding her that they both had other men and women in their lives.

Why that should spoil things she wasn't sure. It wasn't as if Luke and she wanted some kind of reconciliation.

They both knew that could never work. Today they were going their separate ways.

Breakfast was a very perfunctory affair. Luke had already been to a nearby bakery and bought bagels which they had with coffee while they both buried their heads in newspapers. After breakfast they headed straight for the hospital. Luke phoned ahead and was told that Joey had spent a good night and was much brighter and waiting to see them.

Erin was determined to be happy and breezy about Joey's impending departure for Warrapinya. She would satisfy herself that he was on the mend and then she would smile as she waved the two of them goodbye. After that she would be on the first flight back to Sydney where she would get on with her holiday.

But her sang-froid took a dive when they

reached Joey's room and she saw that his bed was empty.

'He might be using the bathroom,' Luke suggested and he crossed to the door of the small en suite bathroom and knocked. 'Are you in there, Joey?'

There was no answer. Luke opened the door, but the room was vacant.

'Perhaps they've taken him for some final tests,' Erin suggested nervously.

'Ssh,' Luke said. 'Did you hear something?'

'No.'

He bent quickly to look under the bed. 'Joey!' he cried. 'What are you doing down there?'

Erin's heart almost stopped with shock. She ducked too and saw Joey huddled on the floor beneath the bed, his face stained with tears. Scrambling on to her hands and knees, she reached out a hand to him. 'Joey, honey, what's the matter?'

The boy's only answer was to burst into more tears.

Horrified, Erin crawled closer. 'Hey, don't cry, sweetheart. Come here.'

'No,' the boy sobbed, bunching tight to withdraw from her.

'What's the matter? Look, here's Daddy. He's come to take you back to Warrapinya.'

The snuffling cries stopped.

Erin shot a dismayed glance at Luke, who was on all fours, peering from the other side of the bed.

'Is Dad really going to take me back?'

'Of course he is, honey.' Erin held out her hand. 'Come on,' she said. 'It's not very nice under here.'

'You promise this isn't a trick? I don't want to go back to New York yet.'

Erin went suddenly cold with fear. 'It's not a trick, Joey. I promise.' Her voice trembled as she tried to sound calm.

'Come on, son,' Luke said gruffly.

In response to Luke, Joey began to crawl forward.

Battling tears, Erin hit her head on the metal frame of the bed as she backed out. She struggled to her feet and Luke was suddenly there to help her. Their eyes met and she saw that he was upset too. He smiled shakily and lifted a hand to tidy her hair. And then Joey emerged from beneath the bed, looking a little shamefaced.

Erin hugged him and, to her relief, he

hugged her back. 'Why did you think you'd have to go straight back to New York?'

'I heard you talking last night. You told Dad I couldn't go back to his place.'

'Oh.' She pressed a hand to her guilty mouth as she remembered the conversation she'd had with Luke, right outside this room when they'd thought Joey was asleep. 'Joey, I'm sorry. I was very upset about your accident when I said that. But I was wrong. I—I want you to go with Daddy. You've got to finish your vacation.'

Joey looked from one parent to the other, his eyes suddenly shining with hope and yet tinged with disbelief. 'You mean it? I don't have to go home yet?'

Erin's throat was so choked she couldn't respond. She'd known for some time that Joey's longing to know Luke was a force to be reckoned with, but this morning she was seeing just how quickly the two had bonded. The strength of Joey's feelings for his father and for Warrapinya scared her. What if Joey could never be happy again living alone with her on the other side of the world?

'Are you going to come with Dad and me?' the boy asked hopefully.

'No, sweetheart. I'm going back to Sydney.'

'Why can't you come with us?'

Erin sighed. 'I've explained this to you so many times, Joey. This holiday is just for the two of you to really get to know each other.'

Joey turned to Luke. 'You'd let Mommy come out to Warrapinya with us, wouldn't you?'

Luke's glance was wary as it flicked to Erin. 'Would you like to come?'

'No, thank you.' She was afraid her son was trying his hand at matchmaking.

'You know you're welcome to join us,' Luke said.

She shook her head. 'It's not what we agreed to. I don't want to poach on your time.'

'Why don't you just come for a couple of days then?' he suggested, keeping his face carefully noncommittal. 'If you see the place again, and see how Joey's settled in, you can set your mind at rest. Then you can be relaxed when you go off to enjoy the rest of your holiday.'

'I—I don't know,' said Erin faintly, but

she was conscious that her will was weakening beneath pressure on two fronts. 'I've left all my clothes in Sydney.' It wasn't a very strong argument. She and Luke both knew that very few of the clothes she'd brought would be suitable for the Outback.

Luke cleared his throat. 'Don't worry about clothes. There are plenty of your jeans and bush shirts still at Warrapinya.'

'Really?' She couldn't believe it. 'I thought you would have thrown those things out years ago.'

His shoulders rose in a careless shrug. 'I never got around to it.'

Her heart thudded as she saw the muscles working in his throat. But his eyes were cool as he let his gaze travel over her and his lips curved into the ghost of a smile. 'You haven't lost your girlish figure. I'd say your old clothes will still fit you just fine.'

To her annoyance, she blushed. Cringing with embarrassment, she turned away from Luke to hide the heat in her cheeks.

Was this how her life would be for the next two days, with her floundering in a sea of confusion and coyness? Was a journey to Warrapinya wise?

If only their son wasn't standing there now, watching them with his big blue eyes wide and his antennae on high alert.

'Joey,' she said, 'you do understand that if I come to Warrapinya it will only be for a couple of days, don't you?'

The boy nodded happily.

'After that I'm going back to Sydney and then to Byron Bay for my holiday, okay?'

'Yeah, that's cool,' the boy said and he grinned at his father.

For a terrible moment Erin wondered if there was a conspiracy in place, but before she could ask another question the nursing sister arrived and it was time to organise Joey's checkout.

CHAPTER EIGHT

How insane was this?

She was going back to Warrapinya, to the one place in the world she'd sworn she would never revisit.

The first time she'd seen these sun-baked plains she'd been an ecstatic new bride, bursting with hope and romantic dreams. She'd burned from head to toe every time she'd looked at her gorgeous husband, had gone weak at the knees whenever they had touched.

Well, if she was honest, she hadn't really changed in that respect. The big difference was that back then they'd touched at every opportunity.

Whereas now…

Now, sitting in Luke's small plane, heading west, Erin's eyes misted suddenly and her throat felt as if she'd swallowed a small mountain.

How naïve she'd been when she'd married Luke. She'd had such a romanticised idea of what it would be like to live in the Australian Outback. Such a dewy-eyed picture—a cosy farmhouse kitchen filled with shelves of colourful home-made preserves, sprigged eiderdowns on beds in lavender-scented rooms, fresh, pure country air filling her lungs as she hung linen on an outdoor clothes-line.

Those things were possible at Warrapinya, but somehow they hadn't seemed quite so alluring once she'd been there, confronted with loneliness and the feeling of not belonging.

No one in the Outback was very interested in costume jewellery—so even her career choice had seemed frivolous and out of place.

She'd tried extra hard to prove to everyone that she could cope. She would be as capable as any Outback woman. She'd always been very well organised, so she'd been sure she'd soon get the hang of managing the homestead and being a cattleman's wife.

Problem was, in the Outback there was so much she couldn't organise. Life there was so dependent on nature. The vagaries of the weather and the land and the cattle ruled everything.

And the distances were so vast. Erin had never got used to that.

After Joey was born she'd been a nervous new mother. She'd wanted to be able to run to a drugstore every time her baby had a sniffle. At home in New York there was a drugstore on every block.

She had been terribly homesick. She had missed her mother and Angie so much.

And Joey had been a difficult baby—he never just ate and slept. And he'd cried so much. He'd had no routine. Erin had always been tired and on edge.

She had hoped when she married Luke that his easy-going attitude would rub off on her but it hadn't. When Luke had shrugged away her concerns about Joey or made a joke of them, she'd just got tenser. It had been so disappointing that Luke hadn't understood what a big deal those worries had been for her.

She'd become neurotic. She realised that

now. Maybe there'd been some post-natal depression involved too. She'd had a million books on baby health and she'd begun to think that Joey had symptoms for just about everything. It had been just awful to be eternally worried about her baby. She'd needed other women to chat to. She'd needed reassurance. Reassurance she could trust—from other women who'd had babies.

She'd befriended Gracie, an Aboriginal woman who lived on the property and was married to Nails. But Gracie had never been blessed with children, so there were limits to how much she could help.

Luke had kept trying to jolly her out of her worries. He'd still thought just about everything could be fixed with a cuddle. But she'd been past jollying.

She had been playing tragedy to his comedy.

And then Luke had seemed to spend more and more time away from the homestead and Erin had begun to think that he preferred working with his cattle to being at home with her.

Eventually it had all got too much for her. She hadn't been able to cope with the isolation and the fears about Joey as well as the loss of Luke's love.

In the end she'd decided she had no choice. It would be better for all of them—for herself, for Luke and for Joey—if she left.

'It won't be long before we're landing,' Luke called over his shoulder. 'If you keep your eyes peeled to the right you'll see the trees along the creek and then the home-stead.'

Swiping at her eyes, she looked out and was surprised that, in spite of her gloomy memories, she felt quite nostalgic when she saw the wandering blue-green line of huge shady paperbark trees that marked the creek. Next she saw windmills set on tall metal scaf-folds and then the faded red tin roof of the low, sprawling homestead, surrounded by paddocks of dull yellow grass dotted with cattle.

Ten minutes later, Luke was deftly landing his twin engined Aero Commander.

There was a cheer squad waiting at the edge of the airstrip. Three little blond-headed, cheeky-faced boys in jeans, checked shirts and cowboy hats were leaping and waving and five Golden Labrador puppies bounced at their feet.

When Joey emerged from the plane a great deal of shouting and peals of laughter burst from the Manning cousins. Almost immediately Joey scooped up one of the puppies and squealed with delight as it licked his face, bump on the forehead and all.

'The doctors took pictures of inside my head,' he told the boys, full of self-importance.

'Did they find a brain?' the eldest cousin joked and all the boys, including Joey, fell about laughing.

'Now, come on, hurry, Mommy,' cried Joey. 'I've got so much to show you. Wait till you see Cassie. She's the puppies' mother and she lets a kitten drink her milk along with her own babies.'

'Oh, my, I can hardly wait,' Erin said.

'Hold your horses, Joey,' Luke called as the boys began to charge off.

The little herd of eager boys and puppies stopped and turned.

'You can't rush off madly the minute you hit this place,' Luke said. 'You've only just got out of hospital. Don't forget, you've had a nasty accident and you gave us all a fright. Your mother and I both had to give up other things we wanted to do just to make sure you were okay, and so far you've got off scot-free. By rights, you should have been in trouble for disobeying orders.'

Chastened, Joey nodded solemnly and the other boys stood by him, looking suitably subdued.

'No running,' said Luke. 'You've got to take things quietly.'

Erin couldn't help admiring Luke's cool command. He had a definite talent for father-hood. There were times when she was too soft with Joey and she could have done with some of that back-up.

But if Luke had been cool and in charge with Joey, he was tense as he walked beside her across the stretch of lawn to the home-stead. Or perhaps it was she who was suddenly tense as they approached the house. Or was it both of them?

They reached the base of the front steps and her insides twisted as she pictured once again the awful memory of the day she left. She saw again the flowers from Luke's bouquet strewn across these timber steps like fallen bodies on a battlefield: fluffy stems of golden wattle, long tubular petals of crimson grevillea, a tangle of dainty purple wildflowers...

Pressing her hand against the sudden ache in her chest, she glanced up and saw a flash of wild emotion in Luke's face.

She wanted to say something, not an apology exactly, but an acknowledgement of the pain she'd caused him, the pain they'd both suffered. But the right words wouldn't come.

And then a woman with corn-coloured hair and a beaming smile came running along the veranda, wiping floury hands on an apron. 'Hello, there,' she called and without any dimming of her smile she held out her hands. 'You must be Erin. I'm Jenny Manning and I've been dying to meet you.'

To Erin's surprise, Jenny hugged her and kissed her, as if they were cousins too.

'Oh, no, I've put flour on you,' Jenny said, noticing a white smudge on Erin's smart navy shirt.

'It doesn't matter.'

'Keith's still out at the mustering camp,' Jenny told Luke, and Erin assumed she was referring to her husband, who managed War-rapinya these days. No doubt Jenny was a perfect Outback woman who coped exceptionally well with her husband's frequent absences.

'Can you show Erin to her room?' Jenny asked Luke. It's made up and ready. I'll take care of the boys.'

With a stern-faced dip of his head, Luke indicated that Erin should come with him down the veranda, but then he strode ahead of her with her small overnight bag and Joey's duffel bag flung over one shoulder and she was forced to follow. Like an obedient dog, she thought, watching his stiff back.

Everything at Warrapinya was familiar and yet different. The sweep of timber-planked verandas with French doors opening on to them were just as she remembered, but the house had been given a coat of white paint and looked fresh and clean. It had always been a cool and comfortable home in a careless kind of way, but now big tubs of ferns had been set along the verandas making it extra shady and inviting.

And there was a wonderfully boy-friendly

construction in one corner—a cubby style tent made from old sheets, quilts, a couple of broom handles and clothes pegs.

Wherever she looked memories lurked, ready to ambush her. So many memories. Bliss and pain. Especially when Luke stopped outside a familiar door and she caught a glimpse of a double bed covered with a quilt in a patchwork of pink, white and blue.

'No.' Her voice was a shaky whisper. 'I can't have this room.'

It had been their room. She'd bought that quilt for their bed before she left America. At the time she'd joked that she couldn't live in a house on a prairie without an American quilt.

She and Luke had shared that bed. *Oh, heaven, how they'd shared it.*

'This is where I told Jenny to put you. She's got it all ready for you,' Luke said gruffly. 'Most of your things are still in the wardrobe.'

'But isn't this your room?'

A bitter smile twisted his mouth. 'You don't think I kept using it after you left, do you?'

Erin struggled to breathe. 'I—I—don't

know what I thought. But I'd prefer another room if that's possible.'

He set her bag beside the bed.

'There's nothing wrong with this one.'

How could he be so insensitive? 'So this is a form of discipline, is it? You won't sleep here, but you expect me to. Why? Because I'm the guilty party?'

A bitter light glittered in his eyes. 'I shifted to another room for purely practical reasons, Erin. A double bed is useful for guests. My parents, for example. They use this room when they come out here. I didn't expect you to have so many hang-ups about where you sleep.'

'Hang-ups?' Suddenly she wanted to hit him. 'Give me a break, Luke. I'm just trying to be—'

She broke off, remembering the fuss she'd made about Luke's spare room in Townsville.

'Let's drop it, shall we?' she said, sounding hopelessly defeated. 'I only enquired if there was another option. This room will be fine.'

Luke was already halfway out the door. 'Do you think you'll be able to find your way about the place if I leave you now to stow Joey's things away?'

'Yes, of course. Where does Joey sleep?'

'On the closed-in veranda with the other boys.'

'He'd love that.'

She could imagine Joey's excitement when he'd discovered he would be sharing that long, dormitory-style bedroom with three other boys. It would be like having a sleep-over party every night. How different from their compact apartment in New York and the urban life he shared with her—just the two of them.

Joey would love everything about this place—boys, horses, puppies…his dad… and, because it was winter, he didn't even have the heat to contend with.

The fear that had gnawed at her since she began this venture resurfaced with a vengeance. Would Joey ever want to come home again? Wouldn't he be lonely with only her for company?

And then she thought…if she and Luke had stayed together, Joey would almost certainly have a brother or sister by now.

But what a useless, unhelpful thought that was.

* * *

Luke charged through the house like a storm trooper.

He was a fool. A first-class fool. He'd been crazy to invite Erin here.

But he hadn't been able to resist the temptation. His burning attraction for her had never died. She was still *The One*. He wanted her more than any woman he'd ever known.

After he'd kissed her in Sydney, after he'd held her at the hospital, all he could think of was how much he needed to keep her in his arms. In his life.

What a hypocrite he was. All the while he was telling Erin off for making a fuss about the bed, he'd been thinking of nothing but grabbing her. He'd wanted to dive into that bed with her and not surface for a week.

These next two days would be hell. He would go mad to see her here, in the home where he'd thought they'd been happy.

Two days. A rueful little laugh broke from Luke. These two days would be fitting punishment for his foolishness.

* * *

The bedroom Luke and Erin had shared was on a corner of the house with windows looking out over paddocks on one side and back to the small cluster of station workers' cottages on the other.

Leaning her elbows on one of the sills, Erin looked out at one of the cottages and saw her old friend Gracie, framed by a window, setting a kettle on the stove.

When she'd lived at Warrapinya she'd been very fond of the shy Aboriginal woman despite the wide gap in their ages and the even wider gap between their cultures.

Many times, when Joey had been restless, the two women had taken turns to pace the veranda with him and then, after they'd got him to sleep, they'd often had a cuppa and a chat.

Impulsively, Erin waved to her old friend now.

Gracie saw her and her face split into a beaming grin as she waved back. Suddenly she ducked and appeared again holding something out to Erin. It looked like a coffee pot. Gracie leaned out of her window. 'Can you come over for a visit?' she called.

Why not? Erin decided. No one would miss her if she paid her old friend a very quick visit.

'Lord love us, Missus Erin!' Gracie's smile was huge as she greeted Erin at her door. 'It's so good to see you. Come in. Come on in.'

Gracie's hair was completely grey now and she looked much older than Erin remembered.

'Sit down,' she said, her dark eyes shining with delight. 'I was hoping I might see you. I even brewed some coffee.' Gracie pointed to the American coffee pot Erin had left behind. 'Every now and then I make coffee for Nails and me—just like you showed me.'

'Wonderful. I'd love a cup of coffee.'

Gracie poured coffee into mugs with great care. 'You know, Nails and I talk about you a lot. We remember how kind you were to us.'

'As I remember, it was the other way round.'

Gracie grinned. 'That Joey of yours is growing fast. He's a fine boy. Going to be as big as the Boss one day.'

'Do you think so?'

'I can tell by the size of his feet.'

'Like a puppy?'

The two women laughed together.

'Tell me what you've been doing,' said Erin.

They were starting their second cup of coffee when the thud of a boot on the kitchen step startled them. It was followed by a large masculine shape filling the doorway.

Luke.

The sense of peace Erin had felt in Gracie's kitchen disintegrated.

'Excuse me for barging in, Gracie,' Luke said and then he frowned sharply as he switched his attention to Erin. 'Everyone's been looking for you.' He sounded more than a little angry and there was an unsettling wildness in his eyes. 'You didn't turn up for afternoon tea and we've been combing the homestead. Joey's in a panic. He thinks you've left us.'

'Oh, goodness.' Erin leapt to her feet. 'I'm so sorry. I didn't realise you were expecting me for afternoon tea. Gracie and I got talking and we lost track of time.'

Luke took a deep breath as if he was de-liberately trying to calm down, and Erin was

more than a little shocked to realise that he
and Joey had both been so worried by her
disappearance.

'Gracie, can I use your phone?' he said.
'I'll let Jenny know. She can put Joey's
mind at rest.'

'Sure, Boss.'

Luke lifted the receiver and snapped a
short message. 'I've found her, Jen. She's at
Gracie's. Tell Joey we're coming.'

'Poor Joey,' murmured Erin. Was his panic
a foretaste of how he would be when she had
to leave? She took Gracie's hands. 'Thanks
for the coffee. I'm so glad we were able to
catch up. It's been just lovely to talk to you
again.'

'Before you go, I've got something for
you.' Gracie crossed to the dresser and
picked up a flat parcel wrapped in bright red
tissue paper. 'Something special.'

'A present for me?' Erin's eyes widened
in surprise.

'When we knew you were coming back
I started making it for you. It's got your
name on it.'

Mystified, Erin unwrapped the gift and, to
her astonishment, discovered a hand towel,

snowy white with green crocheted edging and her name carefully embroidered in one corner.

'You did all this last night?'

Gracie giggled. 'No, Missus. Started it a month back, doing it at night. It took me a week.'

A month ago? Erin frowned and sent a questioning glance Luke's way, but he was staring at the gift with the same kind of surprise she felt. How could Gracie have known she was coming to Warrapinya?

'What's the matter?' Now Gracie looked worried too. 'Did I spell your name wrong?'

'No, no,' Erin reassured her. 'It's perfect. It's a lovely gift. Thank you so much, Gracie. I'm just amazed that you started it a month ago. We only decided yesterday that I would come back with Joey for a couple of days.'

Poor Gracie suddenly looked uneasy. 'It's the old people, Missus. Old Sandy and Uncle Ben. They know the lore and they can see secret things. Sandy dreamed you would come back.' She grinned shyly. 'And here you are. Drinking coffee with me—instead of tea.'

'And the coffee was lovely.' Erin gave

Gracie's wrinkled brown cheek a kiss. 'I'll try to see you again before I leave.'

'Afternoon, Gracie.' Luke gave a brief dip of his head and then turned abruptly.

Erin walked with him back to the main homestead, her mind buzzing. What did the old Aborigines mean? Did they believe that forces beyond her control were at work? That this return to Warrapinya was destiny? The idea both excited and alarmed her.

'Don't try to read too much into what Gracie told you.'

She looked up to find a spark of amusement in Luke's cool eyes.

'You have to admit it's uncanny, Luke. How could those old men know? Why would they dream about me?'

He grinned slowly. 'Sandy collects the mail and he knew that you'd written to me. Maybe the rest was wishful thinking.'

Wishful thinking. Were there people on Warrapinya who wanted her to come back? It was a strangely stirring thought. An impossible thought. She couldn't live here. Taking a deep breath, she said quickly, 'I'm sorry Joey got a fright.'

'Mommy!' Joey's voice called loudly from

the veranda. And then he came running down the steps and zipping across the grass towards Erin. He hurled his arms around her waist, clinging tight. 'I thought you'd gone already.'

'No way.' Wrapping her arms around him, she hugged him to her. 'I was talking to Gracie. You know I'll be here for two days.'

Erin glanced towards Luke. She'd sensed a deeply brooding tension in him that had been brewing ever since they landed. She supposed he was regretting his invitation.

To her surprise, Luke offered to accompany her and Joey when they wandered down to the stables to inspect the famous Raven. But he didn't contribute to their conversation and kept at a distance, so she decided that he'd come merely to keep an eye on his son. Any awkwardness was covered by Joey, who bounced happily between the two of them, filling the gaps of uncomfortable silence with helpful chatter.

After the stables, they walked to the bull paddock, because Joey had to show Erin Warrapinya's massive prize Brahman bull and then they went, via the chicken run and the vegetable patch, down to the creek.

Erin remembered the creek and the way it had been reduced to a mere trickle in the dry season only to regularly flood its banks in the wet. Today there was a moderate flow, a legacy from the previous summer's rain, Luke told her.

Shaded by gum trees and paperbarks, the water looked clear and pretty as it ran over smooth round stones. The banks were covered in soft green grass and at the water's edge there were clumps of longer dark green reedy grass and broad flat rocks.

'Let's take a spell, Joey.' Luke pointed to rocks that were perfect for sitting.

There was a moment of hesitation when Joey realized his parents were going to sit on separate rocks but, to Erin's relief, the boy came and sat with her, nestling close with his head pressed against her breast.

The only sounds were the gentle ripple of the water and the bell-like calls and warbles of birds in the trees overhead. It would have been relaxing if she hadn't been so tensely aware of Luke and the way he sat with his wide shoulders against a tree trunk and his hands resting loosely over bent knees, his cool gaze on her.

'He's nodded off,' he said after some time, and she looked down to see that Joey had fallen asleep, nestled against her.

She settled his head lower on to her lap and stroked his soft hair, pleased to see that the bump on his forehead was already much smaller. And she observed with a kind of detached interest her bare pink and white fingernails. Before they'd left Townsville she'd dashed to the beauty parlour opposite Luke's apartment to have her nail varnish removed and her nails filed shorter so that her hands wouldn't scream City Woman.

She looked back at Luke. 'I'm pleased you wouldn't let Joey get back on that pony just yet,' she said.

He almost smiled. 'Actually, I'm rather pleased he wanted to. There are plenty of kids who would balk at getting back on a horse after coming a cropper.'

'Joey's a gutsy kid,' she replied, letting her motherly pride show. 'And I guess he's stubborn too.' Cautiously, she added, 'Like you.'

Luke's eyes widened just a little. 'Maybe he's stubborn like you,' he said and he smiled slowly—a little sadly at first—but then more warmly so that his smile creased his handsome face and lit up his eyes in an intensely charming way that did terrible things to her insides.

A breathless awareness of all that they'd lost hovered between them in the still afternoon air. The feeling filled Erin's throat so that she had trouble breathing. She was remembering another afternoon when she and Luke had made love down here on the quiet creek bank. She remembered the incredible pleasure of Luke's strong hands bringing her body to fiery life, remembered the heat of their longing, the breathless passion as they came together.

And she knew with certainty that he was remembering it too.

She felt so hot and confused that she found it safer to look down at Joey again.

Eventually she said, 'Joey's had a big day, but if he sleeps too long now we'll never get him to sleep tonight.'

Luke stood. 'I guess we'd better wake him.'

'Hey, Joey.' Erin shook the boy gently. 'It's time to go back.'

Luke stepped on to their rock. Super-conscious of him, Erin stared at his brown leather riding boots and his blue jeans that seemed to go on for ever. And then his strongly muscled brown arms reached down and she felt the electric shock of his hands brushing her thighs as he scooped Joey from her lap.

'Come on, little mate. I'll give you a ride on my shoulders.'

Joey smiled sleepily as Luke lifted him high and Erin scrambled to her feet, her heartbeats hammering madly.

The sun was sinking fast as they walked back to the homestead, and Joey wasn't inclined to talk much. Luke pointed out a group of wallabies grazing near a clump of wattle and he identified birds for Joey—a black falcon gliding in circles high overhead, a flock of pink and grey galahs skimming close above the treetops and a family of star finches busy in the grass.

But while Luke was at ease and happy with Joey, he reverted to being formal and polite with Erin, and she wondered if she'd imagined the wonderful way he'd smiled at her down at the creek.

* * *

After dinner that evening the boys commandeered Luke for a bedtime story and Jenny and Erin sorted out the kitchen.

'The boys just adore Luke's stories,' Jenny said as she stacked the dishwasher while Erin attacked a baking dish with a scouring pad. 'It's a wonder they don't have nightmares, though.'

'Why?' asked Erin. 'Are the stories scary?'

'Yes, but that's what the boys want.' Jenny laughed. 'The scarier the better. You know the sort of thing—daring, edge-of-the-seat escapes from wild animals or bloodthirsty pirates.'

Erin smiled. 'Luke always had an interest in writing fiction, but he never seemed to have time for it. At least, not when I knew him.' She paused in her scrubbing, remembering the day she'd met Luke in New York when he'd been on his way to meet an agent. She'd often wondered what had happened to his dreams of writing.

Jenny's eyebrows arched high with surprise. 'Hasn't Luke told you that he's been writing again?'

'No—no, I don't think he's mentioned it at all.'

Jenny frowned thoughtfully as she closed the dishwasher door and then she stepped closer to the sink where Erin was working. Folding her arms across her chest, she leaned a hip against a cupboard door. 'I know this is absolutely none of my business, Erin, but there's no chance you two might give things another go, is there?'

Heat flooded Erin's face. 'No chance at all. Why would you bother to ask?'

Jenny looked embarrassed and shrugged. 'I don't know. Wishful thinking, I guess.'

Erin worked hard at a black spot on the metal pan. 'Joey's having a wonderful time here. I'm dreading when he has to say goodbye to Luke at the end of this holiday.'

'It'll be harder for Luke. He'll be losing both of you again.' Jenny leaned closer. 'You'll rub your fingers to the bone before you get rid of that spot. It's been there for years.'

Erin stopped scrubbing and forced a half-choked laugh. 'This black spot's probably been there since I burnt the roast. Actually, I did that fairly regularly when I was first married.'

She shouldn't have said that. Suddenly the floodgates opened and she was swamped by another rush of memories. Pictures of herself in this kitchen.

As she rinsed the pan and set it on the drainer she remembered the way Luke would come up behind her when she was working at this sink, the way he'd wrapped his arms around her waist and kissed the back of her neck. She remembered the cheeky suggestions he'd whisper to her and the way she'd flash hot and cold with excitement, and the way she used to lean back into him, relishing the reassurance of his arms about her and the protective shield of his body.

And yet somehow, some-crazy-*crazy*-how, here in this room, in this house at Warrapinya, she'd let that perfect love and perfect marriage self-destruct.

Drying her hands quickly, she tried to pull her thoughts away from that, but suddenly, without warning, her lower lip began to tremble violently.

'Oh, honey.' Jenny threw an arm about her shoulders and hugged her.

Tears slipped down Erin's face. 'I didn't

think it would be so hard to be here with
Luke again,' she whispered.

'I know, I know,' Jenny said soothingly.

Her sympathy was too much. Before Erin
knew what was happening, she was weeping
on Jenny's shoulder, weeping for the
memories of her marriage, and for the way
Luke had looked at her today.

But heavens, she mustn't carry on like this.
Jenny was Luke's cousin—she didn't want to
be sobbed over. Screwing her face tight, Erin
struggled to stem the tears. She forced her
head up, sniffed loudly and took a deep
breath.

'Good grief,' she said in a shaky whisper.
'I don't know where that came from.'

'I do,' said Jenny. 'This reunion has
knocked both you and Luke for six.'

'We shouldn't have waited so long,' Erin
said, and sighed. 'Everything was so strained
when the divorce went through. I took off.
Luke wouldn't talk. I guess it's been hard for
either of us to get over it, because there's
never been any—any sense of closure.'

'Dare I suggest that's because neither of
you really wanted your relationship to end?'

'Oh, no,' said Erin quickly and then, with

her hands pressed to her temples, she shook her head. 'I don't know any more. I feel so confused.'

Stepping back a little, Jenny eyed Erin thoughtfully. 'I'm no counsellor, but I'm sure you should try to have a really good talk with Luke before you leave.'

'What about?'

'That's where I can't help you, because I simply don't know what you need to talk about, but I know Keith and I would have been divorced years ago if we didn't get whatever bugged us out in the open.'

'It's too late for Luke and me to save our marriage,' Erin said. 'Joey's my main concern now.'

'Well, talk with Luke even if it's only for Joey's sake. After all, it's usually the children who end up paying for the problems their parents don't want to talk about.'

'Yes,' said Erin softly. 'I'm afraid that's very true.'

Jenny glanced at the clock on the wall above the stove. 'That bedtime story will be finished. I'd better go and say goodnight to the boys.'

'Me, too. I promised Joey I'd tuck him in.'

Jenny smiled gently. 'You might want to wash your face first.'

'Oh, yes.'

As Jenny bustled off, Erin hurried to the bathroom, wet her face-cloth with cold water and pressed it to her eyes in a vain attempt to reduce the bright pink evidence of tears. Satisfied that it was reasonably effective, she went on to the boys' sleep-out.

Luke was just leaving and he gave her a curt nod. 'Joey's waiting for you.'

Miffed by Luke's tone, which hinted at mild reproach, she breezed past him and bestowed her warmest smile on her son as she sat on the edge of his bed.

'How was your story tonight?'

'Awesome,' he said. 'We had to escape from a tiger shark by swimming through an underground tunnel and then we had supper with mermaids.'

'Oh, my gosh, that does sound exciting.' She gave him a kiss and a cuddle. 'Now sleep tight.'

Her emotions were still running high as she stood looking at the row of beds with their blue blankets and blue and white striped sheets and pillowcases. The four little boys were all clean and sleepy and safely tucked in and she felt very mushy and motherly, as if she could kiss them all. But she knew small boys had a low tolerance for kisses from women who were not their mother.

'Goodnight,' she said and, as the chorus of goodnights faded, she switched off the light and left the room.

The light in the passage outside had been turned out and she didn't know where the switch was. Blinded momentarily, she had no choice but to find her way by stretching her hand and feeling along the timber panelled wall. Two thirds of the way down the hall her fingers touched a belt buckle. Denim. A man's jeans.

She jumped, snatching her hand away. 'God, Luke, what are you doing here in the dark?'

'Just making sure the boys settle down okay.'

'Don't you think I'm capable of settling them?'

'Of course you're capable,' he said gently. 'You're a fabulous mother.'

Adjusted to the darkness now, Erin could

see his face—the heartbreakingly familiar planes and angles, the unsettling light in his eyes, and—oh, help—the shadows and curves of his lips.

'You've always been very good at saying goodnight,' he said and his voice was a lazy, silky rumble. She saw the same look in his eyes that she'd seen down at the creek and a dangerous heat stirred low inside her.

She should keep walking.

But she didn't.

'Erin,' Luke breathed in a husky whisper.

They stood touching close, trembling in the darkness and she couldn't drag her eyes from him. He was staring at her. He was looking at her mouth and his intention was unmistakable. He wanted to kiss her. He was going to kiss her.

Aching need rose through her, blanking out sensible thoughts. She wanted Luke's kiss and her lips parted in breathless readiness.

She couldn't worry any more about whether this made sense. She didn't want to think whether it was right or wrong. She just wanted it to happen.

She wanted Luke to kiss her.

Luke wanted to kiss her.

Slowly, slowly, he was leaning closer.

And she was melting towards him.

He drew her into his embrace and his lips brushed her mouth in a tentative tease that sent flames licking deep. Ah, yes. She was parched earth desperate for rain.

And then Luke settled his open mouth on hers and she sank helplessly into him—into his warm, soft, slow kiss.

Five years. Five long years of separation and loneliness. So long she'd waited. Too long.

'Erin,' he whispered again, making her name sound beautiful, mysterious and special.

I'm here, Luke. I'm here.

She lifted her hands to his shoulders and they kissed deeply, tenderly, savouring each other, letting layer upon layer of memory unfold, so that this kiss felt like a part of every kiss they'd ever shared. Sweet. Hungry. Poignant. Fierce.

Their need and urgency mounted. Erin's hands slipped around Luke's neck and next moment Luke was crushing her mouth, moving his lips over hers with an aching desperation that sent her blood pounding.

His hands slid over her, claiming her, moulding her shoulders, slipping down her sides to the curve of her hips, cupping her bottom, pulling her tightly against him, wringing a soft moan from her.

He trailed kisses over her cheeks, her chin, her eyelids and then he returned hungrily to her mouth.

She matched him kiss for breathless kiss. Everything about Luke felt so right. He had been right for her from the very first moment she'd seen him in Times Square when he'd laid claim to her heart and she'd felt he was her destiny. She'd known then that his arms were created to hold her. His lips were designed for hers. How on earth had she lost him?

How on earth...

Oh, God.

Oh, dear God.

She *had* lost Luke.

She'd left him. They were divorced.

And she should never have come back.

Icy fingers of reality wrapped around her throat, choking her. What was she doing? What was Luke doing? How could they forget that this wasn't right? This was a mistake. Madness. She struggled away from him.

'Erin, come here.' His hands reached for her waist.

She ducked away. 'No,' she cried in a frantic whisper.

He reached for her again.

'What do you think you're doing?' she demanded.

'You know exactly what I'm doing.' He kept his voice low but it vibrated with impatience.

'But we mustn't.' She knew she was overreacting, but she was scared, so scared of falling mindlessly into another huge mistake.

'Why mustn't we?'

'Because—' Breathless and shaking, Erin stared at him. She didn't have an answer so she grabbed the first excuse that came into her head. 'Because you're simply trying to prove Joey wrong—that I don't have a kissing phobia.'

He swore softly. 'And what if I am?'

She cast a frantic glance down the darkened hallway. Were the boys asleep? She and Luke were whispering, but she would hate Joey to hear them. 'You invited me here for two days, Luke. I came here for Joey's sake, and you—'

'I kissed you.'

'You took advantage of me.'

'And you loved it, Bright Eyes.'

A dismayed gasp broke from her. Spinning on her heel, she hurried away from him. He didn't try to follow and once she reached the end of the hall she didn't dare to look back.

She almost ran to her bedroom. And it was only there that she remembered. Instead of thoughtlessly letting Luke kiss her she should have been trying to talk to him. She'd messed up a perfect opportunity to have a mature and meaningful conversation.

Now she only had one day left.

CHAPTER NINE

ERIN spent a restless night. She couldn't lose the feeling of Luke's kiss, the amazing rightness of it, couldn't forget the magic of his arms about her. Couldn't shake off the longing.

She dreamed of him sharing her bed, but when she woke early she found, of course, that there was only an empty space beside her. Looking at the cold pillow that had once been his rightful place she felt a wave of misery sweep over her.

What a mess she was. Today she had to speak to Luke to clarify—

To clarify what exactly?

She wasn't sure, but she knew she had to find a way to let go of the guilt and the regret that still tore at her. She and Luke had to talk about the past five years, to make decisions about the future and Joey and, face to face, they had to find a clear way to let each other go.

Maybe then she would be released from this terrible yearning.

With a soft groan she swept the bedclothes aside and prepared to face the day.

'Joey, have you seen your Dad?'

Erin heard Joey's voice and his bubbling laughter coming from the bathroom and she stopped in the doorway.

Big mistake.

Joey and Luke were standing side by side in front of the basin, both stripped to the waist and with their faces half-covered in white lather. Oh, help. The last thing she needed this morning was a close encounter with Luke's bare shoulders and chest.

'Hi, Mommy,' giggled Joey when he saw her. 'Dad and me are shaving.'

'So I see.' Erin swallowed nervously. The two of them looked so happy together. Father and son. Two gorgeous males. A perfect unit.

Again, as had happened so many times this week, she was guiltily aware of how much

Joey had missed by being separated from Luke.

And again she wondered how Joey would react when it was time to go back to New York with her. She'd told Luke from the outset that there was no chance Joey could stay with him. She was their son's primary care-giver. His mother.

But was she being fair to the boy?

The answer was becoming less and less certain.

Her gaze intersected with Luke's in the mirror. He didn't smile. 'Did you want something?'

'I don't want to interrupt the male bonding session. I can catch you later.'

'No need to dash off. I've almost finished here.'

She didn't mean to stare, but she couldn't help watching the way he tilted his head as he scraped his razor through the white foam, leaving tracks of clean tanned skin.

Almost in a daze, she watched the way his muscles bunched in his upper arm as he worked. And she couldn't drag her eyes away when he shaved the edge of his jaw. Oh, man.

It was such a beautifully masculine action—
the way he jutted his jaw forward and
stretched his neck, accentuating the rugged
bones of his face, the strong column of his
throat.

Another minute and she'd be drooling.

'Joey,' she said, bending quickly to snatch
a damp face-cloth from the side of the bath.
'Why don't I help you to tidy up?' She knelt
beside the boy and wiped the remaining
lather from his face.

'Do you have a shirt?'

'Over there, on the hook with Dad's.'

She helped him into it, pinned on a smile.
'I think breakfast must be almost ready. Do
you want to run along?'

'You coming?'

'In a minute. As soon as I've had a quick
chat with Dad.'

As Joey left she told Luke, 'I'll wait for
you outside.'

'Hang on. I'm done.' Luke gave his jaw a
quick splash with cold water and a hasty
once-over with a towel.

She sucked in her breath as he reached
past her to retrieve his shirt from the hook.

As he shrugged on the shirt and began to

do up the buttons she stepped out into the hallway. Luke followed.

And then, before her courage failed, she said, 'Luke, we really should have a talk before I leave here.'

His grin faded. 'You want to talk about Joey? How we can share him?'

'Well, yes, I guess that's part of it, but—' She drew another breath. 'I think we should talk about us too.'

A dark tinge stained his cheekbones. 'What about us? If you're planning to deliver another lecture about kissing, forget it. I've got the message.'

'It's not that!'

'So what exactly do you want to discuss?'

Erin swallowed. It was so hard to explain, but she knew she had to try. 'To be honest, I—I'm not exactly sure, but I feel as if I'm— as if we're—kind of dangling.'

'Dangling?'

Her hands lifted in a gesture of helplessness. 'That mightn't be the right word, but it's almost as if—as if we haven't really cut loose from each other.'

Luke jerked his gaze away from her to stare across the paddocks of softly shimmering biscuit-coloured grass. 'We're divorced, Erin. We live on opposite sides of the globe. What more do you want?'

Closure.

Chicken that she was, she couldn't quite bring herself to say that out loud.

'Don't you think that after five years of silence there are things we need to discuss? I don't have a particular agenda, Luke. I just think a little communication would be—'

Luke waited while she groped for the right word.

'Healthy.'

A hint of amusement sparked in his eyes, but his mouth didn't twitch into anything remotely like a smile. 'All right. In the interests of healthy communication I'd be happy to talk to you. Two-thirty this afternoon,' he said. 'We can talk in my office.'

Erin's heart was racing like a runaway's when she knocked on Luke's office door at precisely two-thirty.

If everything went to plan, at some stage in the next hour, during a civilised conversation, she and Luke would arrive at the ultimate closure of their relationship.

Everything would be settled and then she would at last be able to step away from her cloud of guilt. Her lingering regrets.

After this talk she would be composed and calm. She and Luke would have negotiated an amicable basis for friendship. For Joey's sake. Her tumultuous emotions would be a thing of the past.

But, more importantly, at the end of this holiday she would be able to take Joey home with a clear conscience, knowing that she and Luke had a plan that would allow Joey to continue to see his father in a friendly arrangement that suited all three of them.

These outcomes were her goal, her focus.

'Take a seat,' Luke said, greeting her with a cautious smile. He pointed to a corner of his office set aside as a conversation area with two dignified brown leather armchairs on either side of a coffee table.

Looking about her as she sank into the luxurious soft leather, she couldn't help noticing how much the room had changed.

Once it had held little more than a desk by a window with a telephone and a computer. Now it was a very businesslike and efficient affair, somewhat at odds with the old-fash-ioned country charm of the rest of the War-rapinya homestead. The large, airy room was painted in rich urban coffee tones. It was equipped with a desktop computer as well as a laptop, two telephones, a fax machine and three filing cabinets.

One wall displayed huge charts of Warra-pinya's cattle grazing system, while another wall housed floor-to-ceiling shelving filled with rows of ring binders, neatly labelled, as well as a library of textbooks and cattlemen's journals. There were also books on script-writing, she noted with some surprise.

'This is different.'

Luke looked about him, as if he was seeing his domain through her eyes. 'I had to get better organised when I built up the business.'

'I take it you've been very successful?'

'I think so. I run three properties these days.'

She almost choked. 'Three?'

'If you remember, I always wanted to expand, and after you left I worked hard. Damn hard. And I had luck with a nicely timed spike in the market.'

He shrugged. 'It was quite a surprise really. I couldn't put a foot wrong. I had to work hard for the first success, but then the others came easily. Two years ago I bought some prime grazing land down near Rockhampton and that turned out to be a stroke of brilliance. And last year I bought another block in the Northern Territory. It's paying its way already.'

'Well done,' Erin said, fearing that her praise sounded hopelessly inadequate. 'You've always worked very hard.'

Luke's eyes narrowed. 'Most people don't consider that a fault.'

'I didn't mean it as a criticism, Luke.'

Frowning, he tapped at one of the copper-toned studs on the arm of his chair. From outside the house came the gleeful shouts of boys and the sharp little barks of puppies as they chased each other across the lawn.

'Anyway, we're not here to discuss my business,' he said. 'We've got some serious communicating to do.' He glanced at her warily. 'Where do you want to start?'

Erin blinked. She was still coming to terms with the busy and successful life Luke had led since she'd left him. He was such an unknown quantity these days. In many ways they were strangers.

It was hard to know the best place to begin.

'Why don't you tell me more about your life now,' Luke said, as if he'd sensed her dilemma.

'I'm not sure there's much left to tell.' Luke knew about her jewellery business with Angie and about her concerns for Joey. He even knew about her former boyfriend, Sebastian.

His grey eyes pierced her. 'Are you happy, Erin?'

Oh, man. Of all the questions he could have asked, this was the hardest. Erin dropped her gaze. Her automatic response was to say of course she was happy. Her life was great.

There were plenty of positives she could share with Luke. She'd found another roomier apartment, almost as nice as the one with the window-seat eyrie. She was surrounded by friends and the familiar buzz and exciting rush of Manhattan. She had a fulfilling, creative career.

She could tell him about days when the

beads and wire and stones she worked with took on a life of their own, guiding her fingers, so that she found herself looking at a beautiful necklace in awe and saying, 'Did I really make that?'

And she could talk about the happiness Joey brought into her life, how their little boy had always been happiness on a stick, bouncing with life, with energy to burn, bursting with curiosity about the world…

Oh, yeah. She could tell Luke she'd managed just fine as a single mom…until she'd discovered the black hole in Joey's world… created by his father's absence.

'Erin?' Luke was waiting rather impatiently for an answer.

'Sure I'm happy,' she said quickly. 'Actually, I'm very happy.'

He was watching her intently, his grey eyes moody and deep. 'I'd say that's the saddest version of happy I've seen in a long time.'

She struggled to defend herself. 'No one's life can be perfect, Luke. We all have to compromise.'

'So what's making those blue eyes so sad?'

She gulped. Time to come clean or this whole discussion was a waste of time. 'You really want to know? You want the unvarnished truth?'

'Yes,' he said quietly.

'Okay.' Taking a deep breath, she stared at her hands, curled rather tightly in her lap. 'I'm carrying a lot of guilt, Luke. There are a bunch of things I'm not happy about. I'm not happy that I couldn't cope better here at Warrapinya. I'm not happy that I made a mess of my marriage, and I'm certainly not happy that my son hasn't known his father or that I've had to bring him up alone. I failed at things that are important to me and that's hard to live with.'

Now that she'd started, the words spilled in a rush, like beads from a broken necklace. 'And I'm not happy that you were so mad at me you retreated into proud, angry silence. I failed there too. I couldn't even have an amicable split with you. There was nothing but silence from you, Luke. Nothing. Afterwards, if I sent you a photo of Joey or a Christmas card, all I got was a freaking reply from your lawyer. And—and—I never quite understood how we actually got into such a mess.'

At first Luke didn't answer. He sat so still he might have been carved from granite. Only the tiny flicker of muscle near his cheekbone gave him away.

'I'm sorry,' he said softly without looking at her.

Oh, God. That was *not* what she'd expected to hear.

His eyes met hers briefly and then he looked away. 'I was so angry and bitter when you left that I couldn't think straight. I was besotted with you, Erin, and I was besotted with Joey, and I'd lost you both.'

Erin pressed a hand to her mouth to hold back a cry. She had to swallow three times before she could speak. 'I'm sorry too, Luke. I know it was terrible the way I ran off without talking to you. I—I think, even though I told you not to, I was hoping you'd come after me.' She forced a weak smile. 'At the time I didn't really know what I wanted. All I knew was I had to get out of the Outback.'

'And that was entirely my fault.'

Another surprise.

His confession set a strange thrumming in her heart. She lifted her head and looked across at him and he sent her the bleakest of smiles.

'I knew how hard it was for you, coming from Manhattan. I knew you wouldn't be able to slip straight into the Australian Outback. But I didn't do nearly enough to help you settle in here.'

'You did warn me that I'd find it hard,' she felt compelled to acknowledge. 'I was the one who pleaded and bullied you into marrying me.'

He shook his head. 'As I remember those weeks in New York, I never gave you a chance to think straight. I couldn't keep my hands off you.'

A bright blush swept up her neck and into her cheeks as she remembered the blazing, limitless passion of those days in Manhattan when her every thought had been centred on Luke. It hadn't mattered then that their lives were based in separate hemispheres. She'd been confident their love would conquer all their problems.

'I was flaming stupid,' Luke said. He looked down at his fist clenched on the arm of his chair and he opened it, spreading his fingers wide. 'You see, we have this bush tradition of tackling tough jobs first up, and I had the crazy idea that if you were going to cope here you shouldn't be mollycoddled. I guess I went too far.'

His mouth quirked in a half-smile. 'Maybe I misinterpreted a comment from my father.'

'What was that?'

Drawing his brows low into an exaggerated beetling frown, he said, 'Just remember, son, you can't have a bed of roses in country that's too tough to grow roses in the first place.'

A helpless little laugh escaped from Erin. 'It might have helped if your father had told me that too.'

'He wouldn't have dared. My mother was totally hung up about interfering in-laws. She wanted to give you space. That's why they stayed away.'

Erin sighed, remembering how Luke's parents had retired to the Gold Coast. Their visits to Warrapinya had been infrequent and cautious when, in fact, she would have been grateful for her mother-in-law's company and support. 'The awful thing for me was that I knew everyone thought I didn't fit in here,' she said. 'And I didn't know what to do about it.'

'You put on a brave face.'

'At first I might have. But then I turned into Annie Anxious.'

'While I played Buffo the Clown.'

Their gazes met. They smiled shyly. Sadly. It was so easy to imagine now that they would do things so much better if they had another chance.

'You were away so much,' Erin said and she held her breath.

'That was the crux of the matter, wasn't it?'

'A capable Outback woman wouldn't have minded.'

'I've never forgiven myself for letting you down.' Luke stared at the floor. 'When I asked you to marry me, I wanted to be the perfect husband.'

Oh, God. That was not what Luke was supposed to say. He was breaking her heart.

'This—this is dangerous ground, Luke.'

'Is it?'

Sure. He was making her want to leap into his lap and throw her arms around him.

But how crazy was that? Even if Luke felt

the way he sounded, even if he felt the way she did, they had to accept that strong emotions—even *love*—were not enough to surmount their huge problems.

Nothing about their situation had changed. She was still a New Yorker and Luke was still an Australian Outback cattleman. They were oil and water—an impossible mix.

'Maybe we should talk about Joey,' she said, struggling to sound matter-of-fact. 'I guess we should work out some kind of arrangement. For the future.'

'Ah, yes. Joey.' Luke offered her an unhappy smile. 'You'll feel less threatened if we talk about Joey, won't you?'

'It's because of Joey that I'm here in Australia, Luke.'

She watched the chill return to his eyes. His throat worked and she knew that he was dealing with emotions as conflicting as her own. Oh, why did their lives have to be such a mess? If only things could be as simple as Joey wanted them to be, with the three of them living together. Happily. Somewhere. Anywhere. Ever after.

'There are a few things I need to explain about my plans for Joey.' Luke spoke with such quiet decisiveness she felt suddenly cold all over. 'I know you don't want anything to do with Warrapinya, Erin, but Joey will inherit my shares in the company and if anything happens to me before Joey comes of age you will have to be involved. In my will I've left everything to you until Joey's old enough.'

'I—I see.' She was suddenly so tense it was all she could say.

'Eventually it will be up to Joey to decide whether he wants to live in Manhattan or to be a man of two worlds. He might even want to come and live here and be a cattleman, and he'd be welcome. It's his birthright.'

'I understand that, Luke. That's fine.' Erin waited for him to continue and, when he didn't, she smiled grimly. 'Where Joey lives when he's an adult is still in the future. It's a long way off. We also need to think about now.'

With both hands she smoothed her jeans over her thighs all the way to her knees.

Luke's eyes followed the movement of her hands. 'What about now?'

She lifted her hands back to the arms of the chair. Took a deep breath. 'I'm worried about the end of this vacation. Joey's so mad about this place he might not want to come home with me.'

She waited for Luke to say something re-assuring, but he didn't. Instead, he stood and walked to the window and looked out. From somewhere out there she could hear the thwack of a ball being hit by a bat and the excited shouts from the boys.

'Joey's going to miss everything about this place,' she said. 'I can't see how he's ever going to settle when he gets back home. But I didn't bring him out here to confuse him.'

Luke kept his gaze on something happen-ing outside. 'Maybe you're worrying unnec-essarily. There must be plenty of things Joey loves about Manhattan.'

'Well…yes.'

'Lots of kids these days have cousins and families spread all over the world.' He turned back to her and smiled sadly. 'We're all one global village, aren't we?'

'I guess.' She sighed, feeling suddenly ex-hausted and drained.

'I could come to New York to visit Joey,' Luke suggested quietly.

'Would you?'

'Sure. I have managers on all three of my properties. I don't need to be here all the time any more.'

'I wish I'd known that. I would have asked you to come before this.'

Luke's mouth tilted in a lopsided guilty smile. 'I should have offered.'

He looked as if he was about to say something more but the phone rang, startling them both.

Crossing quickly to his desk, he answered it. 'John? How are you? Yes, I've been waiting to hear from you. We need to talk about that bull. Just a minute.' He shot Erin a questioning glance as he covered the mouthpiece with his hand. 'Have we just about covered everything?'

No, she wanted to say, but he stood holding the telephone receiver with an air of impatience that suggested that he was eager to be free of her.

Annoyed by the sudden change in him she jumped to her feet. 'I guess we've covered the important things.' She began to walk to the door. 'Thanks for your time.'

'Catch me later this evening if there's anything else.' His eyes softened and he smiled in a way that made her remember again the way he'd kissed her last night.

'Sure.' She sent him a quick, stiff little wave goodbye.

CHAPTER TEN

HER plan hadn't worked.

The peace she'd hoped for hadn't arrived. Erin walked away from Luke's office feeling more edgy than ever, which was just plain crazy considering that Luke had gone out of his way to help her to feel less guilty about their marriage breakdown. And he'd helped to allay her concerns about Joey too. So why didn't she feel better?

From the veranda she scanned the garden, looking for the boys and the puppies, but they'd vanished, leaving their cricket bat lying in the middle of the lawn. No doubt they were having afternoon tea, tucking into the brownies she'd baked this morning. She couldn't face the thought of food.

Turning away from the homestead, she began to walk across the long stretch of pale grassy paddocks that led down to the creek. She walked with her hands sunk deep in the pockets of her jeans and she stared at the ground, her mind too preoccupied to take in the wider landscape.

When I asked you to marry me, I wanted to be the perfect husband.

Did Luke have any idea how she'd felt when he'd said that, now, after all this time?

Once again her eyes and throat began to sting. No, she wasn't going to cry. Not again.

She closed her eyes and drew a deep breath. She'd had unrealistic expectations today—hoping for too much. It wasn't possible to heal five years of pain in one hour's conversation. Now she had to hope that her beach holiday would provide the magic balm she longed for.

Dragging in more deep breaths of fresh air, she walked on and tried to absorb the peace and the stillness all about her—the clean sweep of sky, the silent grass, the shady belt of trees ahead.

When Joe was a baby and she'd felt so isolated she'd found the emptiness and silence of the bush menacing. But now, with four little boys and five puppies bouncing about the homestead, the space and silence provided a welcome sense of peace.

She walked on. She would go as far as the creek and then she'd come back and—

A sudden flicker in her periphery caught her attention. She froze.

There it was again. A sinister dark slither in the grass.

Oh, God, no. Not a snake.

A panicky blast of terror shot through her. It *was* a snake.

Every hair on her body lifted.

Erin had rarely seen a snake up close. Once or twice, when she'd lived here, a snake had crawled on to the veranda to bask in the sun, but Gracie had always been there and she'd dealt with it. Another time she'd seen a harmless carpet snake when she'd been in the bush with Luke and she'd panicked. Badly.

Now she was alone and she was forced to see this creature in horrid detail—scaly, skinny body, ghastly little reptilian head, two nasty beady eyes. Evil, flickering tongue.

And it was way too close—only a yard or two in front of her.

Her legs shook. Her heart thrashed like a

frightened animal trapped in a cage. What could she do? There was no one to turn to. Oh, God. Why had she come out here on her own?

The snake raised its head. It looked menacing. Threatening. It stared at her, flicking its terrifying tongue.

She wanted to run but she couldn't move, couldn't feel her feet. She wanted to scream and scream and scream, but when she opened her mouth no sound emerged. Her blood pounded in her ears. She was sweating. She was going to die. Any second now the snake would strike.

And then out of nowhere she remembered something Joey had told her: *Not all the snakes here are dangerous, Mommy. Brad keeps a pet snake in a tank.*

Somehow, thinking of the boys helped. Joey wasn't frightened to live at Warrapinya. She had to deal with this, had to overcome the terror.

Keeping her gaze riveted on the snake, she took a tiny, tiny step back. The snake didn't try to follow her. She took another careful step back. This time the snake moved too.

Her heart leapt to her throat and she took

three frantic, stumbling steps back before she realised that the snake wasn't coming towards her. It was slithering away, sliding silently, swiftly through the grass.

She turned then and walked as quickly as she dared, remembering that Luke had told her once that if she ran through the grass there was a chance of stepping on another snake.

Just once she looked back over her shoulder. There was no sign of the snake now, so she knew she was safe, but she still kept going as fast as she dared. The stables were to her right and she headed for them.

At last she slumped against the timber wall, her breath coming in frightened gasps and her heart still thumping fit to burst.

She was safe, but it took a few minutes before she began to feel normal. And then she was quite light-headed with relief and she suppressed an urge to laugh hysterically. Wow! She'd confronted a snake. All by herself.

It wasn't as if she'd been brave or anything, but somehow it felt like an achievement. She'd had a minor adventure in the Outback and she'd discovered firsthand that the experts were right about snakes—they were as frightened of people as people were of them.

Wasn't that a significant discovery for a city girl?

Leaning against the rough timber wall, she looked back at the long grassy paddock and she felt unaccountably proud of herself— just a little stronger inside. It would be nice to tell someone about this. Jenny or Gracie would understand.

She couldn't help thinking that if she lived here now it would be different. She would be different. These days she wanted, more and more often, to face up to her fears, to take action rather than to hang back.

Luke would be different too. He had a manager to oversee Warrapinya, a plane, an apartment in Townsville. And Joey would—

'I just need to say hello to Raven, Dad, even if I can't ride her.'

Joey's voice sounded so close she jumped. And then Erin heard Luke.

'You should be fine to start riding her again tomorrow.'

Their voices were coming through the stable wall. She could hear their footsteps on the concrete floor.

'Mommy's leaving tomorrow,' said Joey. 'I wish she could stay here. Why can't she, Dad?'

'She doesn't want to stay.'

'Doesn't she like it here?'

'Not much.'

'Why?'

'It's just the way things are, Joey. Your mommy likes the bright lights. She's a city woman. Some people are country folk and some are city folk.'

She felt bad to be eavesdropping—especially on this conversation. She wasn't sure if she should try to sneak away or let Luke and Joey know she was there.

'I wish Mommy was country folk, don't you, Dad?'

Oh, man. She did *not* want to hear the answer to that question. She opened her mouth, about to call out to them, but then she heard Luke's voice and she couldn't help herself. She had to hear what he said.

'No point in wishing, Joey. You can't make people change. I'm afraid there are lots of things in life you can't change.'

'Like what?'

'Joey!' Erin called loudly. She couldn't

let them continue. She hurried around to the big double doors. 'Hey, Joey, are you in there?'

She blinked as she stepped out of the sunshine into the stables. Joey was standing just outside Raven's stall and Luke was inside it, checking the pony's hoof.

'Hey, Mommy.' Joey waved and looked pleased to see her. 'You missed afternoon tea.'

Luke lowered the horse's hoof, straightened and watched as she made her way towards them.

'I went for a walk,' she said and then she couldn't resist adding, 'I've just had a close encounter with a snake.'

Luke's eyes narrowed with concern. He opened the gate to the stall and stepped out. 'Are you all right, Erin?'

'Yes, I'm fine,' she said breezily.

Luke was watching her with an unnerving intensity. 'What kind of snake was it? What colour?'

'Brown. I'm hoping it wasn't one of the deadly ones.'

'Plain brown or patterned?'

'No pattern that I noticed. Why?'

A worried light flashed in his eyes. He lifted his hand and touched her cheek—ever so softly. 'I hope you gave it a wide berth.'

'I did.' She couldn't help adding, 'But I didn't run.'

'Good girl.'

The tender way he said this and the look in his eyes made her want to curl into him, to feel his arms wrap around her. Not because she was scared any more, but simply because it would feel so good, so right. She was awfully afraid that Luke's arms were the only arms that would *ever* make her feel that way.

Their gazes held. Luke touched her cheek again. His fingertips brushed her skin with tiny feather-soft caresses and he looked deep into her eyes. Her heart beat a drum roll. Her bones turned to liquid as a wave of hot desire rolled upwards from the pit of her stomach. She wanted Luke's fingertips to keep going, to trace every part of her.

Every inch of her skin.

And then his lips could follow where his fingers had been.

'Mommy?'

Oh, good grief. She jerked her gaze from

Luke to Joey and realised he was watching them with wide-eyed curiosity.

Luke lowered his hand and one of the stable doors slammed suddenly. Pieces of dry straw lying near the doorway were swept up and whisked away by a gust of wind.

Tilting his head, Luke sniffed the air. 'I'd say there's rain coming.'

Erin knew rain was always a big deal in the Outback. The three of them went to the doorway to look out to the horizon. A long line of dark purple and grey clouds was rolling in a perfect line across the landscape, moving swiftly towards them like an invading army. Her nostrils caught the unmistakable metallic smell of distant rain on dry earth and she rubbed at her arms as another wind gust swept over them and plucked at her hair.

'Looks like a line squall,' said Luke.

'What's a line squall?' asked Joey.

'You'll soon see.'

'Will we make it to the house or should we stay here?' asked Erin.

Luke grinned at her, his eyes shining with sudden boyish mischief. 'Why don't we sit it out?'

Her stomach did a tumble turn. She knew that look. It was a flash of the old fun-loving Luke of her past, and she knew what he was planning.

'I'll show you,' Luke said, grabbing Joey's hand and urging the boy out into the open. 'Come on, Erin,' he called, but she couldn't follow.

Shaking her head, she watched from the doorway as Luke sat on the dry earth and pulled Joey down beside him. She knew what would happen next and her heart quickened as she watched the huge line of rolling clouds and rain sweeping closer.

'We're going to get wet,' squealed Joey.

'Yeah. Take your shirt off.'

Without waiting for Joey's reaction, Luke peeled the boy's shirt off and then his own. Erin gulped as she saw the play of muscles in Luke's shoulders as his strong bare arms embraced her little son. By now Joey realized what was going to happen too and he gave an excited shout then snuggled in closer to his father.

Luke turned back to Erin. 'Come on, Erin.'

'Come on, Mommy. This is gonna be cool.'

Luke flashed a grin at her. 'Be a devil. For old times' sake.'

She could only just hear him above the roar of the rain as it thundered closer. She could see the excited quiver of Joey's skinny white shoulders as he huddled within the protective curve of Luke's arm. She could picture herself there, with Luke's other arm about her.

She wanted to be there, to join them in the craziness and the wildness. She could remember that other time—being dragged out of the homestead by her excited young husband, being held struggling and laughing on the front lawn as the squall swept down on them—Luke, pulling off his shirt and lifting her blouse to expose their vulnerable bare bodies to the approaching rain.

Now it was Joey's turn. It wasn't her place to be there with them. She didn't belong with them now. That certainty sank inside her, dragging her spirits down and down like a concrete anchor.

'Erin!' Luke held out his hand. He grinned and beckoned to her. 'Come on. Quick!'

The rain was almost upon them. She clutched at the door post, feeling miserable.

She so wanted to join them but it seemed too big a step—an honour she hadn't earned.

But then suddenly, before she could change her mind, she was running—running and squealing as the rain pelted across the dry paddock. She slid in beside Luke like a baseball player reaching home base.

She saw his wide smile, caught the delight in his eyes, heard his whoop of elation and felt his strong arm around her, drawing her in close to his bare chest. Her heart pumped madly.

Lifting his face to the sky, Luke shouted, 'Send her down, Huey!'

'Send her down, Duey!' came Joey's shrill echo.

The three of them linked arms and cheered and squealed as the torrential downpour flattened the dry grass in the paddock in front of them, pressing relentlessly closer. Closer.

It was the most exquisite kind of waiting, like watching a birth or anticipating the touch of a lover.

And then they were lost inside the wall of rain, their bodies shaking with laughter. A kind of wild euphoria engulfed Erin as the cold driving water hit her warm body.

She felt Luke's arm tighten around her and her excited screams blended with his and Joey's as they gave in to the heady exhilaration of releasing themselves totally to the elements.

The squall lasted only fifteen or twenty seconds. It rushed over and beyond them. Soon they could hear the deafening roar of the rain pelting the homestead's iron roof and then it was gone, rolling further inland.

The Warrapinya paddocks were bathed in sunlight once more. Above them the sky was blue.

'Oh, boy, oh, gosh, that was so totally awesome!' Joey was already on his feet, dancing around them with delight.

Drowned-rat wet, shirtless and spattered with mud, the boy looked nothing like the neatly groomed child she'd brought on the plane from Manhattan, but he looked happier than Erin had ever seen him. She felt a rush of love so fierce it hurt.

Her eyes met Luke's and she realised he'd been watching her, his gaze warm and bright.

His hair was damp and plastered to his skull and his bare shoulders were wet and gleaming and he looked way too good. She wanted to touch him, but instead she squeezed water from her drenched hair and then looked down at her own clothes. Good grief. Her cotton shirt was so clinging and transparent she might as well have ripped it off for all the modesty it provided.

And of course Luke noticed. He winked at her. 'How was that, Bright Eyes?'

'Wet,' she said, but she knew her face was giving away her true feelings. She'd been incredibly moved by what had just happened. She'd shared something very special with Luke and Joey—a uniquely intimate moment. A family moment.

But they weren't a family. And she had to remind herself of that as they ran laughing together to the homestead in search of towels and dry clothes.

'Have you told Erin about your film script?'

Jenny directed her question to Luke as she set the dessert on the dining table. She'd gone to special trouble with dinner this evening because it was Erin's last night. First course had been roast beef with all the trimmings and now dessert was a cherry lattice pie with cream.

'A film script?' Erin asked as she passed Luke a generous helping of pie. 'Are you writing one?'

'It's finished,' announced Jenny smugly. 'Finished and on its way to becoming a box office hit.'

'You mean you've actually *sold* a script, Luke?' Erin struggled to disguise her surprise. 'To Hollywood?'

Luke shook his head and frowned at Jenny. 'My loyal cousin is an enthusiast. She likes to exaggerate. All that's happened is an agent has expressed keen interest and he's got a couple of producers looking at it, but who knows? Anything can happen. The movie industry's crazy.'

'But if you've got an interested agent that's wonderful. One of my girlfriends in New York has written a film script and she always says she'd donate her fallopian tubes to science if it would help to get her work noticed.'

Luke smiled wryly. 'I'm afraid I'm fresh out of fallopian tubes.'

Erin laughed. 'Well, dang.'

'What's elopian tubes?' asked Joey.

Erin gulped. For a moment she'd been so caught up in Luke's news she'd forgotten the boys were listening. 'What's the film about?' she asked quickly, hoping Joey wouldn't repeat his question.

'Yanks in North Queensland in the forties, during the war in the Pacific. There's a romance too.'

She sat very still, staring at him. 'It's about your grandparents.'

'Yeah.' Luke looked at his plate and cut off a piece of pie with his fork. 'It's a very simple story really.'

That may be so, thought Erin, but it would probably have all the right ingredients—adventure and poignancy and a nice happy-ever-after Hollywood ending.

Luke had told her about his grandparents on the day they'd met. Right after she'd told him about her parents and the hopeless way their romance had ended. And, shortly after that, she and Luke had headed down exactly the same slippery marital slope.

Crash.

Erin's spoon clattered against the side of her plate. She picked it up, stared long and hard at it. Luke's grandparents' story was incredibly important to him, so important he wanted to share it with the world.

From the very first, when Luke had proposed to her, she'd known that marriage was important to him.

If you come with me, Erin, I want us to be married.

Family was important to Luke.

'Mommy, aren't you going to eat your pie?'

Erin blinked and looked down at the triangle of golden pastry and dark cherries topped with a pure dollop of cream. A few minutes ago the pie had looked wonderfully enticing, but suddenly her throat was so choked she didn't think she could possibly manage to eat it.

CHAPTER ELEVEN

THE night was perfectly still, so still it was hard to believe a rain squall had swept through Warrapinya only a few hours earlier. From the veranda Erin looked out at the black line of trees that marked the end of the silvery paddocks. She looked up at the clear, star-studded sky and saw the red eye of an aeroplane cruising high.

Tomorrow she would be flying away from here. Nails would spend half a day driving her to Cloncurry and then she would catch a commercial flight back to the coast.

In the meantime she had to tell Luke the decision she'd reached.

She sighed heavily, felt panicky—which wasn't good enough. She'd been scared for too long, and by running scared she'd come close to ruining Joey's life. And she'd left a terrible hole in Luke's.

Bringing Joey back to Australia had begun the process of making amends, but now there was another more difficult—oh, so much more difficult step that she had to take.

'Erin, can you spare a minute?'

Luke's voice, coming from behind, startled her. She turned and saw him silhouetted against the lights of the house and she felt a leap inside her, like a flare.

Would she ever develop immunity to this man? It wasn't right to go on feeling this way about her ex.

'I wanted to apologise about the phone call this afternoon,' he said. 'It interrupted us. We didn't get to finish our discussion, did we?'

'We didn't arrive at any long-term plans for sharing Joey.' She hoped she didn't sound nervous.

'Actually, I was more interested in talking about us.'

'Us?'

His face was in shadow but she caught a flash in his eyes that looked suspiciously like amusement. 'What was it you said this morning? Something about dangling?'

'Oh, yes—well—'

'I was wondering if you feel less dangling now.'

Erin swallowed. 'I certainly found it helpful to talk to you about—what went wrong—with us.' She turned back to the railing. It was so much easier to talk about this when she wasn't actually looking at Luke. 'I hope we can keep the channels of communication open now,' she told him over her shoulder. 'It would be nice if we could stay friends.'

'Nice?' He made it sound like a swear word.

'It—it would be helpful for Joey if we were friendly, wouldn't it?'

Luke's answer was to move closer. His hands touched her shoulders and she blushed as she felt the warm pressure through her blouse.

'What about you, Erin? Is that what you want? My friendship?'

Her poor heart thumped. She remembered the way he'd kissed her last night. So much more than friendly. 'I certainly don't want to be your enemy.'

'Are those our only alternatives?' He

dipped his mouth close to her ear. 'To be friends or enemies?'

She was so super-aware of Luke, of his touch and the longing building inside her, that she couldn't think. 'I—I don't know.'

'Wrong answer,' he said and she heard a teasing smile in his voice. 'Now you're going to have to ask me a question.'

'What kind of question?'

Somewhere out in the silent darkness beyond the veranda a lone bird called mournfully.

Luke's hand touched her chin, tilting it gently so that he turned her to face him. She saw a depth of emotion in his eyes that stole her breath. 'Why don't you ask me how I feel about seeing you again? Ask me what it's like to be losing myself again in the most beautiful blue eyes in the known universe.'

She began to tremble. 'Don't flirt, Luke. It's not fair.'

'I can't help it. You're still an incredibly desirable woman, Erin.' He lowered his hands to the railing on either side of her, so that no part of him was touching her but he was there, all around her. She felt light-headed to have him so close. If she moved a fraction of an inch they would be touching and any minute now she'd give in. To resist Luke was asking the impossible.

He dipped his head and let the rough skin of his jaw graze her cheek. 'I've been going crazy just being near you. You've no idea how much I want you.'

Oh, but she did! She was on exactly the same page. Melting hot! Weak-kneed with longing. Already her mind was racing ahead, imagining the two of them naked and passionate in bed together. A whole night of—

Oh, help. She mustn't give in to Luke tonight, mustn't lose her head. It was not the way out of their dilemma. She would only be setting herself up for more pain. She was leaving in the morning. At the end of her vacation she was going back to New York.

She had to talk her way out of this. And fast.

'Sex is not going to solve our problems, Luke.'

'I'm damn sure it would solve the problem I have right now.'

'Don't even joke about it.'

Just minutes ago, she'd been gathering up

the courage to tell him something serious and important. How had she moved from that to being seduced?

'We tried to solve our problems with sex when we were married,' she said, not quite steadily. 'It didn't work then.'

'A lot of things worked, Erin. And we were sensational in bed.'

She closed her eyes, but it didn't help. She was picturing Luke making love to her and she was ablaze with wanting him.

'We were Olympic-standard lovers,' he murmured.

In spite of her tension she couldn't help smiling. 'The duck's pyjamas,' she said, remembering a long- ago conversation.

'No doubt about it.' His lips brushed her ear. 'I've never wanted another woman the way I want you.'

Help! Oh, help! How could a girl withstand such temptation? *Why* should she? Right now all Erin could think was that she wanted Luke to kiss her, to hold her, to make sweet, beautiful love to her.

But we're divorced.

She grabbed at that thought the way a drowning swimmer grabbed at a lifebelt. 'A one-night stand is only going to complicate things,' she said.

'Then stay as many nights as you like.'

Oh, God. She was so tempted.

But then she remembered exactly why his wonderful suggestion was a very bad idea. 'If we become lovers again we would really confuse Joey, wouldn't we?'

Luke went still. He didn't speak. After a tiny beat he wrapped his arms around her and drew her against him, sending an electric tremble through every pulse point. She heard him sigh deeply and felt the rise and fall of his chest.

For a breathless stretch of time she stayed there, basking in the warmth of Luke's embrace, wishing she could go on being held by the man she loved.

If only... Oh, dear heaven, if only...

Gently, sadly, with the kind of unfurling move a dancer makes, she eased herself out from his embrace.

'Erin.' His voice was rough with need as he tried to reach for her again but she took a quick step back.

'No,' she said. 'No, Luke. We mustn't delude ourselves. I couldn't bear to rush in and make the same mistakes as last time. It can't lead anywhere.' Before he could interrupt, she rushed on. 'I'm going away in the morning. Maybe—' She shrugged. 'Maybe after I've had my break at Byron Bay. After you've had more time with Joey and we've both had some space to think. But not now.'

She still hadn't got to the other thing she'd planned to tell Luke tonight, but she was suddenly afraid that if she didn't leave now she might weaken and throw herself at him. 'Goodnight,' she said quickly.

He didn't answer. He just looked at her with a mixture of anger and sadness that ripped at her heart.

She turned and hurried away.

The rest of what she had to tell him would have to wait till morning. Talking to Luke was always safer in daylight.

Long after Erin left, Luke stayed on the veranda staring out into the black bush and the sky. The stars were so bright they looked cheeky tonight. Cheeky and winking at him, winking at his foolishness.

Stay as many nights as you like.

Oh, that was great. That was really smart.

Surely he could have done better than that? Given the fullness in his own heart, the feelings clamouring to be set free, he should have burst into poetry this evening. But he'd been so damn nervous. And maybe a little crazed by desire. Okay, more than a little crazed by desire.

It had seemed to make sense this afternoon in the aftermath of the storm. That was when he'd decided that the best way to win Erin back was to try to seduce her. Once she was in his bed, once he'd spent a whole night making beautiful, impassioned, hotter-than-hot love to her, she'd change her mind about leaving.

And she'd be ready to hear the truth—that he loved her. Still. Always.

He wanted her back in his life.

But instead of seduction, amazingly sensuous romance and confessions of true love, tonight had been a major stuff-up.

Erin had said she wanted space to think and he hadn't said a word. Not a damn word.

Erin paced her room.

It was four a.m. and she couldn't sleep so she'd finished her packing and now she was

ready to leave. Packed and ready to leave—
and still in love with Luke.

Oh, God. There it was. She'd allowed
herself to think the unthinkable. She was still
in love with the man she had married—and
divorced.

It wasn't just a physical thing. She loved everything about Luke Manning. She loved
watching him every chance she could, loved
watching the way he interacted with Joey. And
with Jenny and the boys. The grimness that
had hung over him like a cloud when she'd
first arrived in Sydney had almost vanished
now. Once again he was the easygoing, fun-
loving Luke. Prince Charming in blue jeans.

But what could she do with her love?

With a wail of despair she threw herself
down on the bed, rolled on to her back and
stared up at the slowly rotating ceiling fan.

She'd made the right decision tonight, she
was sure of that. If she'd slept with Luke she
would have begun the whole catastrophe all
over again.

*Would it have been different if Luke had
said he loved me? If he'd asked me to
marry him again?*

Erin blinked and pressed her knuckles to

her eyes before the tears could start. What was the point of asking those questions? Luke hadn't said anything about love. He'd been interested in sex, not re-marriage.

She'd known when she left New York that this journey to Australia was not about mending her relationship with Luke. She'd come because Joey needed to meet his father.

And now, the kindest thing, the best way to demonstrate her love, was to get out of Luke's life so he could concentrate on Joey.

If only there was another answer.

Breakfast was a hurried affair. Erin and Nails had half a day's drive ahead of them before they reached the airport at Cloncurry.

Everyone assembled on the front veranda to say goodbye to her. Jenny was there and the boys, and Joey, of course, watching her with his sad puppy look and Gracie, looking worried.

Luke hadn't appeared this morning and Erin tried not to mind. Perhaps he'd seen her bags sitting on the veranda at the top of the front steps and decided that they were too ghastly a reminder of the last time she'd left.

Reaching into her pocket, she handed

Jenny and Gracie slim packages wrapped in tissue paper. 'They're necklaces I made,' she told them. 'I hope you like them.'

Gracie's eyes brimmed with tears and Erin had to look away. Which was when she saw Luke striding down the veranda.

Her heart trembled in her chest. He looked dreadful, as haggard and sleep-deprived as she was.

Her stomach twisted in knots. This was it. Her only chance to tell him her decision. Aware that everyone was watching her, she hurried along the veranda to meet him halfway.

'Luke, before I leave there's something I wanted to tell you.'

He drew a sharp breath. 'Yes? What is it?'

She pressed her palms together in a prayer-like gesture. 'As you know, I've insisted all along that Joey has to come back with me to Manhattan at the end of this vacation. But I—I've changed my mind.'

'How? What do you mean? You're taking him sooner?'

'I mean—' She looked back down the veranda to the cluster of people waiting to say goodbye to her. 'If Joey really wants to stay here with you, I think he should.'

She heard the sharp hiss of Luke's indrawn breath.

'I haven't said anything to Joey, of course. I think we should just wait and see how the next few weeks pan out, but—I've realised I'd be selfish to drag him back to live in Manhattan if he really wanted to be here.'

Erin held her breath.

'That's—very generous,' Luke said gruffly and then he cleared his throat. 'But—but what about you?'

Her mouth turned square.

I mustn't cry. I am not going to cry.

'I—I would still want to see him, of course.'

'Erin, I know this must—'

'We can work out details at the end of the vacation,' she said, briskly cutting him off. 'If the need arises. I might be jumping the gun. Joey might be quite happy to go back home. I—I just wanted you to know I'm not so black and white on this issue any more.'

'Mommy,' called Joey. 'Nails is coming.'

It was almost a relief to be able to say, 'I have to go.'

The kiss she gave Luke was so quick and frantic she actually missed his cheek and hit his nose. She turned quickly and almost scurried back to the others and the next few moments were a blur as she hurried through the farewells.

'See you in Sydney,' she said, hugging Joey tight.

And then she was down the steps and in the ute and the door was shut. Her tears began to fall as the engine started up.

Nails looked at her with dismay.

'Not again,' he muttered as the ute rolled forward.

'It's different this time,' she blubbered.

'You reckon?'

Nails drove very fast over the bumpy dirt track that cut across Warrapinya to the main road. Probably, thought Erin, because the poor man was desperate to get this over and done with. Sitting beside him in the passenger seat, she couldn't hold back the tears, had no choice but to let them stream silently down her cheeks. She was leaving the two people in the world she loved most.

She had to keep reminding herself that she was leaving for all the right reasons. That was the only thing that stopped her from begging Nails to turn the ute around and take her back.

They climbed a rocky ridge and in front of them the countryside stretched flat and wide all the way to the horizon. The road was a dirt track—a straight red streak cutting across the land and flanked on either side by pale champagne-coloured grass.

Erin dug for a tissue in her pocket, wiped her eyes and blew her nose. 'This is all Warrapinya land, isn't it?' she said.

'Yep. The boundary gate is an hour away.'

Joey's inheritance, she thought, biting her lip. Such a contrast to the crowded streets of New York and her tiny Upper West Side apartment. She thought, for a deeply nostalgic moment, of home. For the first time ever memories of Manhattan didn't pull on her heartstrings the way they always had in the past.

She sighed. 'Gracie told me about the old men who dreamed about me coming back to Warrapinya. Looks like they were wrong.'

Nails frowned. 'That's not the way I heard it. They didn't say you were coming back to Warrapinya. Just back to the Boss.'

Erin drew a deep breath. She mustn't

think about Luke or she'd have some kind
of breakdown.

She tried to remember the meditation ex-
ercises she'd learned in yoga class, but
before she could properly begin the first of
them, she heard the whine of a motor, different from the ute's throaty growl. It came
from somewhere behind her.

'What's that noise?'

Squinting through the windscreen, Nails
ducked his head to get a better angle. 'What
the blue blazes is he up to?'

'Who? What's happening?'

Nails slowed the ute and a small plane
sailed over them, unusually low. 'Reckon
it's the Boss,' he said.

Luke? Her heart leapt to her throat.
'What's he doing?'

'Looks like he's going to land.'

Astonished, Erin watched through the
windscreen as Luke's plane shot over and in
front of them. 'But there's no landing strip.'

'Doesn't matter out here.' Nails brought
the ute to a complete stop and they both
watched as the plane banked in a wide arc
and then zoomed back towards them,
dropping lower and lower.

Erin's jaw gaped. Nails was right. Luke was going to land right on the dirt road in front of them.

Nails was shaking his head and chuckling softly, but Erin sat very still as the little plane touched down with surprisingly few bumps. She couldn't let herself try to think what this meant, wouldn't allow any of her wild and scattered thoughts to take hold.

Luke's plane taxied closer, its twin propellers whirling. What had happened? Did he have bad news from home?

'He's got the little fella with him,' Nails said.

And, sure enough, Erin could make out the small shape of Joey sitting in the cockpit beside Luke, waving madly through a cloud of red dust.

And then her vision blurred, but she managed to see Luke getting out of his seat and moving to the cabin door. She saw his long legs emerge and then he was on the track and jogging towards them.

She fumbled frantically with the door handle. At first it wouldn't open and then it swung free and she stumbled out. 'What is it?' she called to him. 'What's the matter?'

He stopped a few feet away from her. His face was flushed, his eyes fiercely intent.

'What is it, Luke?'

'You can't run away again, Erin. I won't let you.'

She stared at him. *Can't? Won't let you?* What did he mean? Was he going to demand that she come back to Warrapinya? Had Joey thrown a tantrum?

'I'm going to Byron Bay, Luke,' she said with quiet but grim determination. 'You mustn't try to stop me.'

'But I must.' Luke's throat worked and his eyes shimmered in a way that set her heart racing. 'Remember that day we met in New York? I blocked your way then. I made sure I didn't lose you in the crowd. I was crazy to ever let you go. I'm not going to make that mistake again. This time if you go, I'm coming with you.'

Her heart gave a wild little skip, but she tried to ignore it.

'But—Joey wants to be here,' she said.

'Joey wants to be wherever we are, Erin.' Luke tried to smile and failed. He looked suddenly vulnerable, impossibly young and lost. 'I can't bear to lose you again. I love you too much.'

Oh, Luke.

She opened her mouth to tell him that she loved him too, but the sound that emerged was somewhere between a sob and a cheer.

She held out her arms and in the next instant they were together, hugging tight, wondrously tight, as if they were both afraid to let each other go.

Erin could feel their hearts pounding together as they kissed. And between kisses they exchanged thrilled, excited smiles. They laughed, cried a little, kissed again and they held each other with the kind of ecstatic relief that came when a most treasured possession had been lost for too long but was found at last.

With her head against his shoulder, she said at last, 'I love you.'

'I know.'

'I don't think I've ever stopped loving you, Luke. But I haven't been brave enough to tell you.'

'But you have, Erin.'

'Have I?' She lifted her head and looked at him. 'When?'

'It's been there in your eyes. And in your kiss. And just now it was there in the wonderfully plucky way you offered to leave Joey with me.'

'But I should have been brave enough to tell you.'

Luke smiled. Beautifully. 'I should have been brave enough to ask you.'

He kissed her again.

'How can we make this work?' She looked steadily into his eyes. 'I'm not sure I should offer another promise that I could live here at Warrapinya and be happy ever after.'

'I don't expect you to, but I can promise I'd be happy to live with you and Joey in Manhattan, Erin. And I'm free enough to do that now.'

'Are you sure? Would you really be happy there?'

'No doubt about it. I love New York. It's the most exciting city in the world.'

'You'd be able to hassle your agent on a regular basis.'

'That's a bonus I hadn't thought of.'

She smiled wryly. 'But meanwhile, back at the ranch, Joey's learning to love it here.'

'We'll bring him for summer vacations.'

'And you, Luke. You can't just walk away from everything here. I know what it means to you.'

He dropped a kiss on the tip of her nose. 'It'll take time to find the perfect balance, but we will, Bright Eyes. The important thing is that we'll be a family again and we'll work it out together.'

'Yes,' she agreed happily and she released a deep sigh of utter contentment, because at last she knew with absolute certainty that, as long as she and Luke and Joey stayed together, they would find a way to make this second chance work.

Luke drew her close for another kiss, but an excited cheer from behind brought them spinning around.

Their son had climbed down from the plane while they'd been lost in a world of their own and now he was standing near the ute with Nails.

'Hey, Dad,' Joey shouted, with a grin that stretched from ear to ear. 'Mommy does like kissing you after all.'

Ah, yes… they were a family again.

MILLS & BOON®

Live the emotion

Tender romance™

HER OUTBACK PROTECTOR by *Margaret Way*

When Sandra Kingston inherited Moondai cattlestation, overseer Daniel Carson was ready to support her. Daniel was strong yet gentle, a heady mix for a young woman who had been forced to fight her own battles. Having Daniel close by her side made Sandra feel both protected…and desired.

THE SHEIKH'S SECRET by *Barbara McMahon*

Laura has been swept off her feet by a gorgeous new man! But Talique is torn. Laura doesn't know his real name, the past that drives him, even that he is a sheikh! And just as his plan is about to be revealed he realises that his intentions have changed: he wants Laura as his bride!

A WOMAN WORTH LOVING by *Jackie Braun*

Audra Conlan has always been flamboyant and wild. Now she will repent her mistakes, face her estranged family – and evade men like gorgeous Seth Ridley. But when her past threatens her new life, can Audra forgive the woman she once was and embrace the woman she is meant to be?

HER READY-MADE FAMILY by *Jessica Hart*

Morgan Steele is giving up her city career and moving to the country! When handsome Alistair Brown meets his new neighbour, he thinks she is a spoilt city girl. As Morgan gets close to Alistair and his daughters, she realises that what she has been looking for is right under her nose…

On sale 2nd June 2006

Available at WHSmith, Tesco, ASDA, Borders, Eason, Sainsbury's and most bookshops

www.millsandboon.co.uk

**Through days of hard work
and troubles shared, three women
will discover that what was lost
can be found again...**

Tessa MacCrae has reluctantly agreed to spend
the summer helping her mother and grandmother clean
out the family home. They've never been close, but
Tessa hopes that time away will help her avoid facing the
tragedy of her daughter's death and the toll it's
exacting on her marriage.

At first, the summer is filled with all-too-familiar
emotional storms. But with the passing weeks each of
their lives begins to change. And for the first time,
Tessa can look past the years of resentment.

**'This much-loved family saga of insecurity and
tragic loss is compulsive.'**
—*The Bookseller*

19th May 2006

FREE

4 BOOKS AND A SURPRISE GIFT!

We would like to take this opportunity to thank you for reading this Mills & Boon® book by offering you the chance to take FOUR more specially selected titles from the Tender Romance™ series absolutely FREE! We're also making this offer to introduce you to the benefits of the Reader Service™—

- ★ **FREE home delivery**
- ★ **FREE gifts and competitions**
- ★ **FREE monthly Newsletter**
- ★ **Books available before they're in the shops**
- ★ **Exclusive Reader Service offers**

Accepting these FREE books and gift places you under no obligation to buy; you may cancel at any time, even after receiving your free shipment. Simply complete your details below and return the entire page to the address below. You don't even need a stamp!

YES! Please send me 4 free Tender Romance books and a surprise gift. I understand that unless you hear from me, I will receive 6 superb new titles every month for just £2.80 each, postage and packing free. I am under no obligation to purchase any books and may cancel my subscription at any time. The free books and gift will be mine to keep in any case.

N6ZEE

Ms/Mrs/Miss/Mr...Initials ....
BLOCK CAPITALS PLEASE

Surname ....

Address ....

....

....Postcode ....

Send this whole page to:
The Reader Service, FREEPOST CN81, Croydon, CR9 3WZ